D1493995

THE

ROWAN

TREE

Book Two of the Toby and Sox Trilogy

THE

RONAN

TREE

Book Two of the Tribe and Fox trilogy

THE
ROWAN
TREE

Book Two of the Toby and Sox Trilogy

PAULA BRODERICK

Illustrations by Dave Leonard

Matador
9 Priory Business Park,
Wistow Road
Kibworth Beauchamp
Leicester LE8 0RX, UK
Tel: (+44) 116 279 2299
Fax: (+44) 116 279 2277
Email: books@troubador.co.uk
Web: www.troubador.co.uk/matador

ISBN 978 1848767 973

British Library Cataloguing in Publication Data.
A catalogue record for this book is available from the British Library.

Typeset in 11pt Book Antiqua by Troubador Publishing Ltd, Leicester, UK

Matador is an imprint of Troubador Publishing Ltd

Printed and bound in Great Britain by TJ International Ltd, Padstow, Cornwall

MIX
Paper from
responsible sources
FSC
www.fsc.org
FSC® C013056

To Nigel, Lee and Simon.
Thanks for all the help and encouragement.

The Inner World

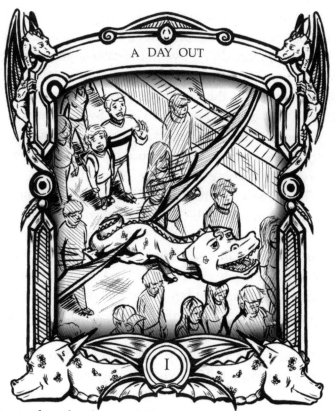

A DAY OUT

I

It was the school summer holidays and Toby was bored, his friend Harry was away somewhere, he had hardly seen anything of his Dad, Edward, since he had started his new job a few weeks before, and his Mum, Sally, was busy in the garden. Toby could see her now, from his bedroom window, she was kneeling down picking strawberries, part of him knew he really should go and offer to help, but the rest of him just couldn't be bothered. He fell onto his bed with a sigh, what was he going to do?

He toyed briefly with the idea of going through the tunnel under his bed to the Inner World, but even if he did, he knew he would probably still find himself alone. Sox, the dragon, didn't live in the cave anymore and it was a long journey to Ffain's castle up on the High Mountain. Plum, the Christmas fairy, spent most of her time in the Valley of Jewels and as for Swift the unicorn, well, he and his herd could be just about anywhere. Toby sighed again and stared up at the ceiling, it seemed everyone was doing something except him.

There was a scuffling noise, Toby sat up as a mouse ran out from under the bed. It stopped and regarded him from the middle of the room. Toby stared at the mouse, and the mouse stared back; it looked just like any other mouse …, could it be? Another mouse scampered out and sat beside the first one; but this one was different, it was fat and round and had a cheeky expression on its face.

"Ernie!" Toby exclaimed. "Oh, it is good to see you, if only you could tell me what's going on."

The rainbow mice were the only creatures that travelled between the two worlds regularly. In the Wide World they looked just like any other mouse, but when they returned to the Inner World they became brightly coloured, each mouse changing to a different colour every time; which made it very hard to work out who was who; but tubby little Ernie, who hardly ever said a word, was always easy to spot.

Toby knew the rainbow mice couldn't speak to him once they left the Inner World and became more like their earthbound cousins, but that didn't mean they couldn't communicate with him at all. The slim mouse waved one paw in the air to make sure Toby was watching, and then moved the paw up and down Ernie's back, from head to tail, drawing small triangles in the air.

The boy guessed straightaway, "A dragon, something about a dragon?"

The mouse pointed to its feet.

"Sox. You mean Sox."

The mouse nodded and then balancing up on its back legs, it held one front paw out to each side and began to flap them up and down.

"Flying? Sox is flying, that's wonderful news."

The last time he had seen the little dragon, Sox had just been given his first flying lesson by his father, Ffain the green dragon and ruler of the High Mountain. It had not been a success; in fact, poor Sox had crash landed into a lake.

Toby was beginning to enjoy the miming game, now the mouse simply pointed to the floor.

"Oh dear, he hasn't crashed again, has he? Has he hurt himself?"

The mouse shook its head, stamped a back leg, pointed back to the floor, and then round the room.

"I'm sorry, I don't…" Toby began. "Oh hang on, is it here? Do you mean here?"

The mouse nodded, and Ernie grinned.

"Sox is coming here!" Toby was delighted. He wondered when Sox would arrive, but there was no way of finding out. Still, at least he knew he was on his way; something was happening, at last. The mice were still looking at him expectantly, Ernie rubbed his tummy.

"Oh, of course, I'm sorry. Just wait there, I won't be a moment."

Toby ran downstairs into the kitchen and took a biscuit from the larder. He was almost back at the door, when he remembered how large Ernie's appetite was, and went back to the larder for a second one.

The mice seemed very pleased with the biscuits, Ernie managing to eat all of his and a good third of his companion's. Before they left Toby asked them to tell Sox that he would definitely be in, waiting for his friend to arrive. With a wave of farewell the mice scurried back under the bed, and silence settled on the room once more; but Toby felt a lot happier now, at last something was happening. He crossed over to the window and looked down into the garden; perhaps he would go and help Mum, after all.

As it turned out by the end of the day, two things had happened.

Firstly, Edward had arrived home earlier than usual, and announced to Toby. "Tomorrow, we are going to have a day out, a boy's day out; just the two of us. I'm sorry I haven't had much time for you lately, but things have settled down with my new job now, and as Mum's going to be busy making jam, I thought it would be fun to spend the day together."

"That will be great," said Toby. "What are we going to do?"

"There's somewhere special I want to take you, and I've got something to tell you." Edward winked at him, and Toby knew immediately what his father meant.

Even though it had been weeks since Toby had discovered that his father had also been on an adventure in the Inner World when he was a boy, because of the pressure of his new job Edward still hadn't told Toby about it.

"I want to wait until we've got time," he had said. "I don't want to have to rush, there's a lot to take in, and it's important that you understand. Besides, I want to gather my thoughts, it was a long time ago and I've never been able to tell anyone about it."

Toby had understood; the Inner World was a secret that could only be shared by those few who had been lucky enough to go there; even Mum didn't know. The rest of the Wide World seemed to have forgotten all about dragons and unicorns, and it was best things stayed that way.

Edward refused to tell him any more about their destination, just saying that he wanted it to be a surprise, but when he knew Sally wouldn't overhear, he did add, "Bring Sox, if he's around, he'll enjoy it too."

The second thing that happened was the arrival of Sox. Toby had been up to check his bedroom several times during the rest of the afternoon and evening, but it wasn't until he was lying in bed that night, about to go to sleep, that the green and purple dragon put in an appearance. The little dragon crawled out from under the bed, exhausted, dishevelled and so out of breath he could barely speak.

"Flew," he puffed. "Whole way…not counting the bits I walked between crashes…will tell you all about it later."

He collapsed on the bed next to Toby.

"Sox, I'm so glad you're here, and you're just in time. Dad's got something planned for tomorrow; he's taking us somewhere special."

"Tomorrow...oh good," mumbled Sox, and fell fast asleep.

They set off early the next morning, Sally had made them a picnic to take and Toby took his rucksack along, so that Sox, who always shrank in size when he came through the tunnel, could sit in it and look out when they got to wherever it was they were going. Edward was still being very mysterious, refusing to give any clues as to their destination; all he would tell them was that it was going to take a while to get there.

Meanwhile, Sox told Toby all his news; the little dragon had been very busy catching up with his education, which had been somewhat lacking due to his being brought up by the rainbow mice instead of his parents, after his absentminded mother, Petunia, had mislaid Sox's egg. Apart from flying, Ffain had been teaching him that being the ruler of the High Mountain entailed a lot more than just guarding

the pass to the Back of Beyond, all of the creatures relied upon the green dragon and his family to ensure that their part of the Inner World was a safe and secure place to live.

Sox recited the dragon code of chivalry, "Courage, honour, justice and the readiness to help the weak."

"A very noble sentiment, by which to live your life," Edward commented. "If only more people lived with such regard to others, the world would be a better place."

"What about breathing fire?" asked Toby. "How is that going?"

"Well, it's not as simple as it looks," Sox replied. "It's all in the breathing; there's quite a technique to it. Dad has given me some breathing exercises to do, so I just have to keep practising, when I've got the time. But so much has happened in the last few weeks, Mum has been teaching me about trees and plants, Ebony has been explaining the day to day running of the castle, honestly Toby, it's nice to come and see you and have a bit of a rest."

Toby smiled at him.

"It certainly sounds as though you've been very busy."

Ebony was a black hare and Ffain's donzel. All of the dragon rulers had a donzel to see to the day to day running of their castles. Traditionally, this job was always done by black hares; they were helped by teams of white hares, known as nippies, who performed all the menial tasks.

"Nearly there," Edward called out. "Look ahead – now!"

7

They came over the brow of a hill and the sight that lay before them rendered Sox and Toby speechless. The road ahead forked and in between laid the remains of a huge stone circle. Some of the stones had fallen down but several remained upright, and it was easy to make out the original outline of two circles, one within the other.

"It's the Story Circle!" Toby exclaimed, as Edward turned onto the right hand road following a sign that read, 'Stonehenge. Car Park'.

Sox was trembling with excitement.

"It's just as Magenta told us."

Magenta, a rather overweight and slightly mad red dragon, was the guardian of the Valley of Jewels. Toby and Sox had met her when they had been on the quest to find Petunia, Sox's mother. Magenta, or Auntie Madge as she liked to be called, had given Toby and Sox their first lesson in dragon history explaining how, thousands of years ago, humans and dragons had lived peacefully together. Indeed the dragons had helped the humans in so many ways; their lives would have been very difficult without them. The humans and the dragons' favourite pastime was to spend their evenings together sitting round a roaring fire telling each other stories and legends. The people held the dragons in such high regard they decided to build a huge stone story circle in their honour. With the dragon's help they had succeeded and, it was obvious to Toby and Sox, this was what they were looking at now.

Sadly the harmony between the humans and the dragons had been destroyed by the murder of Topaz, a yellow dragon, who had been falsely accused of causing a fatal avalanche. Topaz's husband, Lucifer, had gone on a revengeful killing spree that had resulted in the humans banishing all dragons from the Wide World and, over time, the existence of dragons had faded from the people's memories. As punishment the other dragons had sentenced Lucifer to exile in the Back of Beyond.

"Can we go in? Can we touch it?" asked Sox eagerly.

"We are certainly going to go in," said Edward, as he negotiated the car into a parking space. "But I'm afraid you're not allowed to touch it. You can see for yourselves how many visitors come here. It's far too old and precious to allow everyone to climb all over it."

There were indeed a lot of people, coach loads in fact, and the car park was almost full. Toby was most surprised.

"Do they all know about the dragons?" he asked as he helped Sox into the rucksack and then lifted it carefully onto his back.

"Where's it gone? I can't see it."

Sox turned his head from side to side from his vantage point up on Toby's shoulders.

"We have to go through a tunnel under the road to get there," Edward explained. "And no Toby, none of these people will know about the dragons. This site has been examined by historians and archaeologists for hundreds of years and none of them can explain what it is, how it was built, or why it is here. Interesting, eh?"

They joined the end of the queue to buy entry tickets.

"Got your mascot with you, I see," the man in the

booth said when it was their turn. He nodded at Sox, who was poking up out of the top of Toby's rucksack, and sitting very still. "You're in luck, we're not charging for dragons today."

"I should think not, seeing as they helped…"

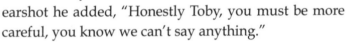

"Come along Toby," Edward interrupted, giving the man some money and taking their tickets. "Let's not hold everybody up."

Once they were out of earshot he added, "Honestly Toby, you must be more careful, you know we can't say anything."

"Sorry Dad," Toby hung his head in shame. "But you must admit it was a rather stupid thing to say, not charging for dragons."

"I agree," said Sox quietly in Toby's ear.

Edward smiled, "Pretty annoying, I must admit. Now, before we go through the tunnel, do you want to take an audio guide? It's a handheld recorder that you listen to and it tells you what is known about the history of the site; or would you rather walk around and look without one."

"I'd rather walk around and remember what Magenta told us," Toby replied.

"Good, so would I. I like to try and imagine it the

way it was, and it is still a very special place, despite the crowds."

Edward led the way, Sox was very surprised by the tunnel which was large enough for several people to walk through  upright at one time. The only tunnel he had experienced before was the one under Toby's bed, this was very different. As they emerged there was a drawing on the wall depicting teams of men hauling huge blocks of stone, obviously someone's interpretation of how the circle had been built; Sox tutted with disapproval, not a dragon in sight.

It was a clear sunny day but quite windy, a strong breeze tugged at their coats as they walked up the slope out of the tunnel and saw the stone circle lying before them.

"Wow," said Toby. "It's huge!"

They followed the path that led around the site, for a while no one spoke as they each tried to picture Magenta's description of the Story Circle and combine it with what lay before them. They came to a bench and Edward suggested that they sit down.

"Can you imagine it, Toby?" he asked. "Can you picture it in the dark, a fire burning in the middle, the people sitting round in a circle and then the dragons encircling them, lying against those huge stones? There would have been singing and storytelling, the people laughing, everyone so happy, content in each other's company. The people felt safe because the dragons were their friends and would protect them from wolves, bears or any other dangers that came along. It must have been such a wonderful time, and the Old Ones, the ancient dragons, were very wise, the people trusted and respected them. What a shame it all had to end the way it did."

"Why did it happen, Dad?" Toby asked sadly.

"Well," his father gave a sigh. "I suppose the people felt they didn't need them anymore. It wasn't just the dragons; they turned their backs on nature, on living in harmony with the world. Humans built bigger and bigger cities, society became more complicated, and they forgot about the simple things. The country people, the people of the mountains and wild places, remembered but the townspeople looked down on them and laughed at their simplicity. Dragons became a thing of legends, stories to frighten naughty children with, but I think maybe they did feel a little guilty after all about Topaz, because soon the existence of real dragons was denied all together."

While his Dad was talking Toby had been aware of Sox wriggling around in the rucksack, trying to get a better look at the Story Circle, and getting quite irritated with the other visitors who kept passing in front of where they were sitting and blocking the dragon's view. Suddenly several things seemed to happen at once, the wriggling stopped and Sox's weight lifted from Toby's back, something green and purple shot over their heads, blown, it seemed by the wind, and headed over the barrier towards the centre of the stones.

"What on earth is that?" a lady, standing nearby, asked her husband.

"I'm not sure," he replied. "It could be a balloon, or maybe it's a plastic bag. What a shame people don't take more care of their rubbish, look the wind is going to blow it right into the middle."

Toby and Edward jumped to their feet and then stood as still as the stones themselves, watching Sox's flight in horror. The little dragon seemed to be struggling with the wind as he bobbed up and down, to and fro, before finally dropping into the stones and disappearing out of sight.

"What on earth does he think he is playing at?" Edward muttered under his breath, as he and Toby began to make their way through the onlookers. "Quick, let's get round to the other side, the path's nearer the stones there."

People were talking and pointing as they pushed their way through the crowd, constantly glancing across to the centre to try and catch a glimpse of Sox. Just as they reached the

spot where the path was closest to the stones, Toby heard someone shout, "There it is."

He looked up just in time to see Sox fluttering up and heading towards them.

"Don't worry, I've got it," Edward called out lunging past a young man, who was just reaching up to catch the dragon. "Just some rubbish," he said, smiling round reassuringly at the crowd as he unceremoniously stuffed Sox back into the rucksack and buckled it up firmly. "We'll take care of it."

"It didn't look like rubbish," the young man began uncertainly.

"There's a bin just over there," someone else pointed out helpfully.

"That's okay," said Edward. "We'll take it home and get rid of it, er, recycling you know. Come along Toby, let's go."

Edward marched off with Toby hurrying along behind, not a word was spoken until they were safely back in the car and Toby lifted the flap of the rucksack to reveal a grinning Sox. Then they all began talking at once.

"What on earth did you…?"

"Why did you…?"

"That was absolutely brilliant, I was there Toby, I was there. I sat in the middle of the Story Circle, and it was as if I could feel the Old Ones."

Sox was so excited neither Toby nor Edward had the heart to stay cross with him.

"Just promise me," said Edward. "That you won't do anything like that ever again."

"I promise," said Sox, as he winked at Toby.

"Right then," Edward continued. "I suppose we had better get on. I was going to get a cup of coffee, but I think I'll forget that for now. There is somewhere else I want to show you, a very important place. I thought we would have our picnic there and I can tell you all about it, it's to do with your father."

He smiled down at Sox.

"He wasn't always great at thinking things through before he did them, either."

They left the open plains and travelled through the countryside for about an hour before Edward announced, "Nearly there, can you see what it says on the sign?"

"White Horse Hill 3 miles," Toby read as they turned right at a crossroads.

The surroundings here were a lot prettier; they were driving through narrow lanes with thick hedges, which allowed the occasional glimpse of fresh, green fields. Every now and then they came across picturesque villages containing quaint cottages; one village even had a duck pond in its centre.

As they turned up yet another small lane Edward

said, "Look over to your left, can you spot anything on the hillside?"

Toby and Sox tried to peer over or through the hedge as the car began to climb uphill. "I can see something white up there," said Toby.

"So can I," Sox agreed. "But I can't make out what it is."

"Here we are," said Edward, driving into a car park and parking. "Now, I know there's a notice board over there, but I want you to come with me first. We are going to walk across to the viewpoint, then there's a particular place where I want us to have our picnic. I'll tell you the whole story there and when we come back you can look at the notice board and read what the experts have to say, okay?"

Toby carried Sox in the rucksack again and they followed Edward, who had the picnic things, through a gate out of the car park. A sign by the gate pointed across the grass, right to 'White Horse' and left to 'Viewpoint', they turned left and walked downhill to the corner of the field.

"Just look at that view," said Edward, pointing ahead. "Isn't it amazing? You can see for miles, look you can just make out the Cotswolds over there and, over that way, that's Oxford; but it gets better, follow me."

The view was fantastic; the land fell away steeply below them and then opened out into a broad, flat plain, covered in a patchwork of fields and villages. Edward turned following the hedge, the field rose up sharply on their right and they could just make out the top of another hill rising above it.

"I can see it again," Sox called out excitedly from his

vantage point. "Look Toby, there it is, the white thing we could see from the car. Whatever is it?"

"I'm not sure," said Toby, stopping beside his father.

"Is it a horse?" he asked remembering the signs they had passed.

"So they say," said Edward, pulling something out of his pocket. "This will help, I bought a picture taken from the air. It really is the best place to view it from. Can you see it now?"

Looking at the picture it was obvious to them that it was indeed an enormous white horse carved into the hillside.

"Gosh, it's gigantic!" Toby said. "You must be able to see it for miles, but who made it Dad? What's it for?"

"That's what I am going to tell you. You see that hill there?"

Edward pointed to a small but very steep hill that rose up to the left of the one bearing the white horse. The top of the hill was completely flat as if it had been cut off, and on the top there was an area of bare ground which stood out, it and the white horse were the only things around not covered in lush green grass.

"That," Edward announced, "is Dragon Hill."

"What!" Toby exclaimed.

"Dragon Hill," Sox repeated, round eyed with astonishment. "Named after a dragon, a real dragon?"

"Oh yes," said Edward chuckling at the effect his words had had on them. "A real dragon for sure – your Dad!"

"Ffain!"

"Dad!"

Edward laughed again.

"Come on, that's where we are going to have our picnic, on Dragon Hill. It's the perfect place for me to tell you Ffain's story; hopefully you'll be able to picture things as I speak."

They set off up the field, Sox couldn't take his eyes off Dragon Hill as Toby and Edward walked to the top and out into a lane. The little dragon just couldn't think why his father would have been in this place. What on earth could have happened to bring him here?

"We're right below the white horse now," said Edward, pointing to the hillside rising almost vertically on his right as they turned to go down the lane.

"We just have to walk a short distance along this road and then we can climb up onto the hill."

It wasn't far, down the lane, around a bend and there was another gate; beyond which a series of steps had been cut into the steep slope leading to the top. Soon they were sitting there, in the sun, with the edge of the white horse just visible above them and the sweeping panorama of the vale below; and Edward began to tell them Ffain's story.

PART 1. A SOLEMN OATH

After the dragons were banished from the Wide World the lions declared that they would become King of the Beasts. The unicorns disputed this and a terrible war broke out between them. As the humans had turned against the dragons, and they knew the unicorns were the dragons' friends, most of them supported the lions; but the people of the mountains and wild places still remembered the old days, they liked the dragons and unicorns, so they chose to fight on the side of the unicorns.

There is an old nursery rhyme that commemorates it.

The lion and the unicorn were fighting for the crown,
The lion beat the unicorn all around the town.
Some gave them white bread, and some gave them brown;
Some gave them plum cake and drummed them out of town.

Since their banishment the dragons had allowed most of the portals between the two worlds to fall into disrepair, and the locations of those that were left were only known to a privileged few. These were used by the unicorns injured in battle; they came to seek help from Lavender, the purple dragon, who was a healer; she would tend the unicorns' wounds and nurse them back to health.

The dragon had set up her healing sanctuary in a lush meadow by a bend in the river. It was a very peaceful place, the river was broad there and slow moving, it flowed smoothly over the gravelly river bed creating a soothing sound. There were willow trees for shade and plenty of fresh grass for Lavender's patients.

The two adult purple dragons, Horatio and Lavender, and their daughter Petunia, lived in the foothills nearby in a large but cosy cave that overlooked the sanctuary, so that Lavender was always on hand whenever she was needed. Compared to the grandeur of Ffain's castle and Magenta's palace, the purple dragons lived very simply. Horatio was a famous plantsman and, before the dragons were banished from the Wide World, he and Lavender went on frequent expeditions collecting rare and exotic species. It was Horatio who had created the wonderful gardens in the Valley of Jewels, where the red dragons lived. When the planting was completed he went on to fill the gardens with beautiful birds and insects and on one occasion had even arrived home with Neville, the last dodo in the world, who now lived in safety on an island in the lake at the Valley of Jewels.

During their travels Lavender had been able to meet other healers and collect many medicinal plants; and now she was putting her knowledge to good use with the help of a team of nippies that she had trained.

When her parents were travelling Petunia had spent her time in the Valley of Jewels growing up with Magenta and Aralu, the orphaned son of the yellow dragons Topaz and Lucifer. They were all cared for by Magenta's parents, Rufus and Ariadne. But Petunia much preferred to spend time with her parents, helping Horatio to tend his plants and learning the art of healing from her mother.

The nippies had built some shelves in the entrance of the purple dragon's cave and this was where Lavender stored her supplies of herbs and medicines. Mother and daughter would pass many happy hours here, hanging up bunches of herbs to dry and grinding seeds into powder, before storing them carefully away until they were needed.

At this time Ffain was a fine, young dragon, very nearly fully grown and well trained, by his father Lochinvar, in the arts of combat and chivalry. Ffain would come down to the valley to visit the unicorns in

Lavender's care. He would hear the news of what was taking place in the Wide World and he became increasingly frustrated about not being allowed to go and help them. Again and again Ffain begged Lochinvar to allow him to enter the Wide World and help the unicorns in their fight, but his father always refused.

"The people have banished us, and we swore we would never return to the Wide World. A dragon's word is his bond, Ffain, and it cannot be broken. I am sorry for our friends the unicorns but they know they are welcome to come here at any time. The lions would not follow them into the Inner World; the unicorns should just come and live here peacefully with us," he said.

"But why should they be driven from their homelands? They didn't want to go to war," the young dragon replied angrily. "It isn't fair father, why should the lions just decide they're in charge, they are no better than anyone else."

"I'm afraid it is often the way of things," Lochinvar answered with a sigh. "There will always be bullies wanting what someone else has got. I wonder how long it will be before the humans tire of the lions and send them off to live in some remote place. They are a strange race. Who knows," he continued with a snort of amusement, "maybe one day they will even regret sending the dragons away."

Ffain decided to have one last try.

"Father please, just tell me where the portal is. No one else will even know I am gone; in fact you wouldn't even have to let them know you told me, everyone would just think I had found it by myself. We can't stand by and let our friends be treated like this, it's not chivalrous."

At these words Lochinvar turned on his son with a roar.

"Chivalrous! Chivalrous! Don't you dare talk to me about chivalry, you expect me to break my word, lie to the other dragons and then you have the cheek to mention chivalry. Get out of my sight!"

Ffain couldn't remember ever seeing his father so angry; he flew out of the castle and down the High Mountain, coming to rest at the fork in the path above the Valley of Jewels, where he sat down to think things through. Despite his father's anger he was still determined to go and fight with the unicorns. He racked his brain trying to think of a way of discovering the whereabouts of a portal.

He had already asked all the adult dragons and it was pointless asking again. He knew the rainbow mice still travelled between the two worlds and he had spoken to them, but all of the portals they used were far too small for a fully grown dragon to squeeze through. He had tried asking the injured unicorns but they too were sworn to secrecy, even though they admitted to him that they were in danger of losing the war unless they got some help, but still they would not break their word.

Ffain banged his fore paw against a nearby rock in frustration, how could all the others just sit back and do nothing? There must be a way; there must be something he had missed. Ffain began to go over everyone again in his mind, Magenta and Petunia were far too young, they wouldn't know anything. Aralu was the same age as him, but seeing as he spent most of his time alone in the hills, the chance of his overhearing anything was fairly remote, and, as the unicorns always arrived during the night; it would be impossible for him to try and watch to see where they appeared from.

He thought of the adult dragons again. How could they let this happen? He just couldn't understand their behaviour especially as he knew how hard Lochinvar, Rufus and even old Horatio had fought for justice and tried to make peace with the humans during the incident over Topaz and Lucifer. For the dragons to send one of their own kind into exile had never been heard of before but even though they had taken this drastic action, and despite their pleading, the humans wouldn't see reason and had forbidden all dragons to ever enter the Wide World again.

That was it! That was it! Ffain leapt to his feet with excitement, how could he have been so stupid? It was obvious; there was one dragon he hadn't asked, one who surely couldn't quibble about chivalry – Lucifer. All he had to do was go into the Back of Beyond, find Lucifer and ask him.

Without waiting to think any more about it Ffain flew back up the mountain towards the pass guarded by his family's castle. Hoping that neither of his parents happened to be looking out, he flew quickly pass the castle and landed on top of the mountain to speak to the sentries. Lochinvar always had two of the swiftest

nippies
posted
here. Their
job was not
to allow
anyone to
pass either
in or out,
but Ffain

knew there was one exception.

"Good morning," he said as he landed, trying to appear casual.

"Good morning Sir," one of the nippies answered respectfully. "How can I help?"

"Lavender has sent me to collect some quiver tree roots for her. One of the unicorns is gravely ill and she cannot leave its side."

"I'm very sorry to hear that, but haven't you forgotten something?" the hare looked at Ffain quizzically.

Oh no, thought Ffain, don't tell me there's a password or something. He tried not to appear flustered, "Er, no I don't think so."

The nippy smiled up at him, "Your collecting bag Sir, you've forgotten your collecting bag. Left in a bit of a rush did you?"

Blast, thought Ffain, how could I have been so stupid? He only realised he had spoken out loud when the hare spoke again.

"Not to worry Sir, Mr. Horatio often does the same thing, so often in fact he keeps a couple of spare bags here. Can't think of everything in an emergency, can you? Just hold on a tick and Bobtail will get one for you."

He gestured to the other nippy who hopped behind some nearby rocks and then reappeared carrying a canvas bag.

"Here we are Sir," said Bobtail handing the bag to Ffain. "You're in luck; it's not far to the nearest quiver trees, so it shouldn't take you too long. See you later."

"Y-yes," stammered Ffain, hardly able to believe his luck. "I expect I will, bye."

The dragon spread his wings and flew off from the top of the mountain. The land fell steeply away and he could see the path of the pass below him as it wound its way down the steep mountainside. In front of him as far as he could see lay a monotonous desert of sand and broken rocks. In the distance he could just make out a clump of quiver trees, they appeared to be the only living thing in the whole desolate place. For no reason, other than he could think of nothing better to do, he flew towards them.

He landed in their sparse shade and tried to think of a way of finding Lucifer. He knew he had to find him quickly or the nippies on sentry duty would become suspicious and raise the alarm. But how was he going to find him? Where could Lucifer be in this vast inhospitable place? Ffain shifted uncomfortably, the sun baked ground was so hot it was beginning to burn his paws.

What a terrible place, imagine having to live here. Of course, that was it. If you had to live there you would need shade and water, if he could find those, he felt sure he would find Lucifer.

Ffain spread his wings and took to the skies once more; he flew up higher and higher, circling round and round as he scanned the land spread out before him. On the far horizon he could see the distant outline of another range of mountains. He hadn't known there were mountains on the other side of the Back of Beyond; they were a long, long, way away. He hoped Lucifer wasn't there; he didn't have time to fly that far. He circled round again looking towards the foothills of the High Mountain when he caught a glimpse of something out of the corner of his eye. A patch of blue! There appeared to be a patch of blue lying on the desert floor. Then he realised, of course, it was the sky's reflection in a pool of water.

Ffain flew over to it, and then began to fly a low circuit around the water's edge. There! He spotted what he was looking for almost immediately, a trail of paw marks leading back into the nearby hills. Ffain followed them, landing where they disappeared into the space between two large boulders.

He stood still, listening, there was no sound and nothing appeared to be moving, but he had the uncomfortable feeling that he was not alone. Someone or something was watching him. There was a slight scuffling noise and he turned his head quickly in its direction, but there was nothing to see. He caught a movement from the corner of his eye and swung his head the opposite way just in time to glimpse a flash of red before it disappeared between some stones.

He heard the noise again, louder this time and coming from above his head. Ffain looked up and saw a line of small, bright red creatures staring down at him from a ledge of rock. They were scorpions; they regarded him menacingly, holding their sharp pincers defensively in front of their bodies, their poisonous, stinging tails curved over their backs, ready to strike. The dragon kept his distance realising that, as small as they were, there were a lot of them, a big enough dose of their poison could prove fatal, even to a dragon as large as himself.

Would he be able to breathe enough fire to kill them all before he was stung? How many of them were there, anyway? Ffain stared at the scorpions as he tried to work out what to do next. A row of beady eyes stared back. They must be protecting something, but what? Surely it could only be one thing. Ffain took a deep breath and called out in a commanding voice.

"Lucifer, I need to speak to you."

Silence.

"Come out Lucifer, I know you're there."

Silence.

Ffain swallowed his pride.

"Please Lucifer, I need your help."

There was a moment's more silence and then a voice,

croaky with disuse, answered him mockingly.

"What? Do my ears deceive me? Is this Ffain, son of the mighty Lochinvar, asking for help from the most despised dragon in two worlds? Be gone, leave me in peace, I have nothing to say to you."

At the sound of their master's voice the line of scorpions moved forwards to the edge of their rocky platform, waving their barbed tails. The noise of their feet scuttling across the hard surface made Ffain's skin crawl, and he tried not to flinch.

"You may well have nothing to say to me, but would you not like to hear news of your son? Show yourself Lucifer so that I can at least tell Aralu that I have seen his father."

The silence that followed was long enough for Ffain to fear that he had failed in his quest. He knew that he would have to return to the pass soon, he was just about to turn away when the sound of movement came from behind the boulders.

Lucifer the yellow dragon came slowly into sight; he was still a mighty dragon, larger than Ffain, as big as Lochinvar; but his golden scales were dull, his huge wings dry and dusty, his claws torn and dirty.

At the sight of their master several of the scorpions made their way over to him and, climbing up, began to run over his body. Ffain shuddered as he realised they were grooming him. Lucifer smirked at the green dragon's obvious distaste.

"You see Ffain, I am not without some friends, even in this forsaken place. They have their uses, don't you my pretties?"

Lucifer smiled down at the scorpions, before readdressing himself to Ffain.

"They keep an eye on things for me; let me know if anyone or anything is about; not that I get many visitors, of course. They bring me titbits now and then, help keep the place tidy; not as efficient as a team of nippies, but they do their best."

"You mean you share their carrion?" Ffain asked with disgust.

"Well, it helps to vary the boring diet your father deigns to provide for me."

"It is no different to what we eat ourselves," Ffain replied defensively.

Lucifer waved a dismissive paw.

"So, have you satisfied your curiosity? Will you tell my son how well his father is looking?"

"Do you have a message for him?" Ffain asked.

An evil gleam came into Lucifer's red eye.

"I can't believe you flew all this way just to exchange pleasantries. What do you want? Tell me why you are here?"

Realising that this was probably his only chance to acquire the information he needed, Ffain tried to pick his words carefully.

"After the dragons left the Wide World the lions declared themselves 'King of the Beasts'."

"Really, how interesting," Lucifer interrupted. "I don't expect that will last long."

Ffain continued.

"The unicorns won't accept their rule, they are fighting a war with the lions and I'm afraid they're losing. I want to – I must go and help…"

"Hmph, how honourable of you. Typical do gooding green dragon, just like your father. So why don't you  go then? What's stopping you?"

Ffain suddenly felt foolish and rather embarrassed.

"Um, I can't find…um, no one will tell…", he stopped, took a deep breath and began again.

"I don't know where the portals are. They've been closed you see, since you, um, since the incident. None of us, Aralu, Magenta, Petunia or I, not one of us knows where they are. I know there is at least one still open because the unicorns arrive in the valley to be treated by Lavender. I need to know where it is, I have to go and help."

"I see," said Lucifer with a slightly amused look on his face. "How resourceful, good old Lochinvar, he really is a dragon of his word, isn't he? But why should I help you, what's in it for me? What can you do for me young Ffain, that is the question."

Lucifer regarded Ffain coldly with his evil red eyes but the green dragon held his gaze bravely.

"I suppose you want to be like your father, don't you?"

Ffain nodded without breaking eye contact.

31

"And I also suppose that one day you will take his place, when dear Lochinvar goes to live with the Old Ones, you will become the guardian of the kingdom."

"Yes, that is true," Ffain answered steadily. "But not for many years yet, I hope."

Lucifer regarded Ffain for a while; the green dragon could tell he was thinking something over and he stood quietly knowing that this was his last chance. Finally Lucifer appeared to make a decision.

"If I tell you the location of a portal, I want something in return. You Ffain, must take an oath. You must promise me that when you become the guardian of the High Mountain you will release me from my exile and allow me to return and live with my son. You must swear this oath on the heart of the White Dragon."

Now Ffain did utter a gasp of surprise and dismay. To swear an oath on the heart of the White Dragon was the most binding promise a dragon could give. It could never be broken. Surely to give Lucifer back his freedom and allow him access to the rest of the Inner World would not be possible.

"Oh no, this can't be true, please tell me this isn't true, Mr. Edward. Surely my father would never make such a promise?" Sox was so disturbed by Edward's story he started to pace around the picnic things in agitation.

"Calm down Sox, please," said Edward, catching

the thermos flask just before it toppled over after being hit by the dragon's tail. "You must understand Ffain was a lot younger then, he had been brought up to believe that it was his duty to fight against injustice. He was desperate to go and help his friends and he couldn't understand why Lochinvar wouldn't allow him to."

"How old was he, Dad?" asked Toby. "It's difficult to understand, I know dragons live a long time and that they don't measure time in the same way we do."

"Yes, you're right, time passes in a very different way in the Inner World. In human terms I suppose a dragon must live to be, oh, somewhere between 1,200 and 1,500 years old."

"What!" gasped Toby in surprise. "But that's ancient. So how old was Ffain when this all happened?"

"Oh, I suppose he must have been about six or seven hundred years old and Lochinvar and Lucifer would have been about a thousand. I know Horatio and Lavender were older and Magenta and Petunia were younger, but I'm not sure by how much."

"But surely Dad would never have done such a thing?" asked Sox, who was still looking extremely worried.

"But you don't know that he did," Toby pointed out. "After all Lucifer isn't free, is he?"

"Oh no, of course not," said Sox with relief. "I hadn't thought of that. He couldn't have promised, could he?"

The little dragon turned back to Edward.

"Well, let me finish the story and then you'll find out."

"Just one more thing Dad; who was the White

Dragon? I've never heard of a white dragon."

"I'm not sure, maybe Sox can explain."

Toby and Edward looked at the little purple and green dragon, Sox gave a small shrug.

"Some say it's just a myth but if the White Dragon did exist it was the mightiest, noblest and wisest ruler of them all and an oath sworn on the White Dragon's heart can never be broken. If there was a White Dragon it disappeared a very long time ago and no one knows what happened to it or its kin; but no dragon would take that vow lightly," Sox gave Edward a worried look. "It can't be broken, it's a solemn oath."

Although Ffain had lived all his life knowing that one day he would become the Guardian of the Kingdom, he had never given much thought to when that day would actually come. Lochinvar would live for a long, long time yet, and when he did grow old, well, so would Lucifer. Ffain knew the two dragons were about the same age. It was too far ahead to even think about seriously. The unicorns needed help now and besides, if he went to fight he may not even come back. What was your promise worth then, if you were dead?

Ffain suddenly became aware of something else, the shadows around him were lengthening, time was passing. How much longer would the sentries wait before raising the alarm? The green dragon raised a front paw and, placing it on his chest; he looked straight into Lucifer's terrible red eyes as he spoke.

"A vow forever and a day,

On the White Dragon's heart.

Let all who witness hear me say,

Until death's fatal dart.

When I, Ffain, become the Guardian of the High Mountain I will grant you your freedom Lucifer, you have my word. This is my solemn oath."

Lucifer nodded and smiled with satisfaction.

"I look forward to the day Ffain, I look forward to the day," he smirked.

Ffain gave an involuntary shudder as he heard these

words and he felt a moment of panic. What have I done, he thought, what have I done? But Lucifer spoke again and his words drove all doubt from Ffain's head.

"And to prove *I* am a dragon of my word, you will find what you seek behind the waterfall that lies below the crossroads between the Valley of Jewels and the High Mountain. Now be off with you and leave me in peace."

PART 2. THE BATTLE OF DRAGON HILL

III

It was the end of the day by the time Ffain reached the waterfall, a place he had passed by many times without giving it a second glance. Now, however, he examined it more closely and realised, just as Lucifer had promised, it was possible to pass behind the fall of water that cascaded down over the rocks and enter into a tunnel.

It was almost dark as he emerged cautiously into the Wide World and looked around. He found himself standing beside a rowan tree on top of a small, but steeply sided, hill; another much larger hill rose up almost vertically in front of him, blocking his view. Behind him the last rays of the setting sun revealed a vast view over miles of countryside, all of which appeared to lie peacefully in the gathering dusk. No point in looking in that direction, then, he thought.

Grateful for the covering darkness, Ffain spread his wings and flew up and over the towering hillside. What he saw as he cleared the top of the ridge, took him so much by surprise, he almost tumbled from the sky. Below him were hundreds of men labouring in the semi darkness, digging an enormous, circular trench, in what, Ffain quickly realised, was an effort to defend the top of the hill. They were building a fortress, a rough and ready one maybe, but a fortress none the less. Ffain also spotted something that made his heart soar and brought him down from the sky. It was a flag bearing a dragon, a red dragon, against a green and white background. Ffain landed neatly beside it causing the man, who stood next to it, to jump with shock, his hand automatically reaching for the sword by his side.

"Good grief!" he exclaimed. "Where on earth did you spring from? No, don't bother to answer that, I haven't got time. Just tell me, have you come to help? I hope so because things are getting desperate here."

Ffain took to him immediately; he was obviously used to being in command, straight to the point, and with no time to waste.

"Yes. My name if Ffain and I have come to do whatever I can. I'm sorry it has taken me so long to get here, and I'm sorry I am alone. I'm afraid the others won't break their vow."

"That is only to be expected," the man replied. "I won't ask you why or how you have managed to come, but I am glad you are here. I am King Uther Pendragon, as you can see my men are digging in; we plan to defend this hilltop to the last.

"I'm afraid you are almost too late, the unicorns have been defeated, and they are in full retreat. My son, Arthur, is fighting a rear guard action to try to protect them and allow them to escape, together with their wounded. They are on their way now; we plan to hold the enemy here, so they can use the portal on the next hill. You have arrived just in time, my friend; we need your help badly.

"If you fly to the south you will find them, I was about to send a messenger, but you will be swifter than any horse. Please tell Arthur he can begin to fall back, by the time he and his men get here we will be ready to make our last stand. I just hope we are not too late to save some of the unicorns. Go well, my friend."

Ffain needed no further urging, he felt a surge of admiration for Uther, and he recognised the king for what he was, a mighty warrior, willing to stand up for justice and fair play, until the end. The green dragon spread his huge wings and rose into the air, flying low over the countryside in the direction Uther had indicated.

He had only travelled a short distance when he saw them, a herd of unicorns together with a small troop of men on horseback. A few miles further on Ffain could just make out the pursuing army of lions and people, a much larger force, marching forward with deadly intent. Ffain could see the unicorns were exhausted, some of them wounded, and their progress was much slower than their enemies. He spotted Uther's flag amongst the men and flew down.

The men looked up in amazement at his approach, some of them began to cheer, and Ffain heard a voice calling out, "At last, at last!"

A tall young man approached him and introduced himself as Prince Arthur; Ffain gave him Uther's message adding. "It's not far now, you're almost in sight of your father's fortress."

Arthur grinned up at him with relief, "It's good to hear that and we could certainly do with your help. I'm not sure we can move the unicorns any faster, many of them are wounded and their comrades refuse to go on without them. I have never come across such brave and honourable warriors; they have been hopelessly outmatched by the lions and the people marching to their standard. Even strong hooves and sharp horns are not much use against claws, teeth and arrows. We have tried to help as much as possible but we are hopelessly outnumbered, the only thing that has been in our favour is speed, but they are slowing down dreadfully now. Still, they refuse to leave anyone behind and I can't blame them, they know what fate awaits them. I'm ashamed to say that unicorn horns are highly prized amongst certain men. And all they wanted to do was live in peace."

Arthur shook his head sadly, but his natural

optimism soon reappeared and he looked up at Ffain with a smile, saying, "But with your help we should be able to hold them and buy the unicorns the time they need."

A magnificent unicorn with a golden horn limped slowly towards them. He was bleeding profusely from terrible wounds to his flanks, a young unicorn paced beside him, with obvious concern.

"It's Ffain, son of Lochinvar, isn't it?"

Ffain nodded.

"I am Zephyr, and this is my son Sirocco. I know your father well, and I can't begin to think how you managed to persuade him to allow you to come, unless, of course, he doesn't know you are here."

Zephyr realised the embarrassment his words had caused and gave a snort of amusement.

"I had to come Sir; I couldn't stand by and do nothing. My father ..."

Zephyr interrupted Ffain's explanation.

"Your father is a dragon of his word, he promised the humans that no dragons would enter the Wide World again, *he* has kept that promise."

Ffain dropped his head in shame at Zephyr's words, but still couldn't help feeling resentful towards his father for putting him in such a position.

"However," the unicorn continued. "He has managed to be of great assistance to us in our struggle."

Ffain's head shot up and he looked at Zephyr in astonishment.

"How, what has he done? He hasn't come...?"

"No, no, no, he sent his donzel, Sable and some of

his nippies. The nippies have been a great help guiding our wounded back to the portal, and as for Sable, he has been of enormous assistance to us. No one can move across the land as swiftly and as furtively as a hare, especially a black hare. He has proved to be indispensable, spying on our enemies and keeping us informed as to their whereabouts. Why without him I believe our escape route to the portal would have been cut off. Don't you agree, Arthur?"

"Yes, his help has been invaluable. Thanks to Sable, we have been able to come here by a roundabout route, buying my father time to construct his defences and, I believe the lions still have no idea where the portal is situated."

Ffain was crestfallen, he had had no idea that Lochinvar was playing a part in the unicorn's fight for freedom, and he certainly hadn't noticed Sable's absence from the castle. He felt rather stupid when he remembered the things he had said to his father.

Seeing the look on the dragon's face Zephyr took a step closer to him and said, "No matter what has taken place between you and Lochinvar, I am very pleased you are here. Your presence may very well save the day."

The words were barely out of the unicorn's mouth before his legs buckled and he sank to the ground.

"Father!" Sirocco called out in alarm.

"He is suffering from loss of blood; we must try to staunch his wounds. No, my friend," Arthur held up his hand to silence Zephyr as he tried to reassure his son. "Do not speak, save your strength."

Arthur turned to Ffain.

"I have an idea, but I need your help, we must buy time to allow Zephyr to recover. I just wish there was some way we could stem the bleeding before it is too late."

An image of Lavender nursing the unicorns back in the valley, flashed into Ffain's mind.

"But there is," he said. "We just need to find some cobwebs; there must be some around here somewhere. If we apply fresh cobwebs to the wounds it will stop the bleeding."

"I'll go," Sirocco volunteered. "I'll get the other unicorns to help, we'll soon find some. Just hang on father, I'll be back shortly, I promise."

Zephyr raised his head as his son cantered off into the darkness.

"So much courage in one so young," he said weakly. "If it hadn't been for him charging and goring the lion that attacked me, I wouldn't be here now."

Arthur laid a hand comfortingly on the unicorn's neck.

"Ssh, be still, save your strength."

He turned back to Ffain.

"We need to fool the enemy and make them think we are camping here for the night. They won't want to attack in the dark; they will be more than happy to wait till daybreak. If I get some of my men to make some piles of wood could you breathe on them and light several small fires? The lions will assume they are our campfires. Meanwhile, I will continue to move as many unicorns and men as I can up to the fortress and the portal. Zephyr will have to stay here; hopefully before dawn he will have recovered enough to complete the journey. I hope that by the time daylight arrives we will all be up at the fortress and our enemies will realise they have been held up by nothing more than a series of bonfires. Can you do it; can you keep the fires burning all night to fool them?"

"Of course," Ffain assured him.

And so the long night began, Ffain helped the soldiers gather wood and started several small fires in the surrounding area. These were soon mirrored in the distance by the campfires of the lions and their followers, as they prepared to bed down for the night. Ffain was shocked to see how much closer they were than when he had first spotted them earlier that evening.

The dragon lit one fire near the place where Zephyr lay. Sirocco had returned earlier, his horn covered in cobwebs gathered by the faithful unicorns for their leader. Ffain had placed the sticky webs over Zephyr's wounds, patting them gently into place, relieved to see the flow of blood slowing down almost immediately. Sirocco kept watch over his sleeping parent, and Ffain would snatch a few words of conversation with the young unicorn every time he passed by on his endless rounds of fire tending.

They talked mainly about the Inner World, Sirocco being keen to learn all he could about his future home. Ffain tried to find out more about how Sirocco had saved his father's life, but the unicorn was reluctant to discuss the incident, just saying modestly, that he knew Ffain would have done the same thing if his father had been in mortal danger. Ffain's admiration for the unicorn was tinged with a little envy for the experiences he had undergone; even though Ffain recognised

this as being illogical. But the blood of warriors ran through the green dragon's veins and he couldn't help but look forward to whatever the coming morning would bring with more than just a little eagerness.

Meanwhile, Arthur and his men continued to stealthily move the remaining unicorns on through the night, towards King Uther and safety.

There was the faintest lightening in the eastern sky when Arthur arrived back at Zephyr's side. A rest and some sleep had restored a lot of the unicorn's strength, indeed, in many ways he appeared in better shape than his comrades, who had spent a sleepless night carrying out their allotted tasks.

"It's time to move," Arthur said softly. "Do you feel up to the journey?"

Zephyr got slowly and painfully to his feet, Ffain was relieved to see that the cobwebs were working, having formed a large scab over the wound.

"I'm ready."

They set off in the direction of the ridge, the trail was easy to follow, having had so many feet and hooves pass over it during the night. Arthur led the way, Ffain and Sirocco walked on either side of Zephyr, ready to assist him should he stumble or fall. No one spoke, Zephyr concentrated on putting one hoof in front of the other, the rest of them followed, almost unable to breathe as they silently willed him forwards. The sky lightened slowly as they walked.

Arthur was the first to speak, pointing ahead and saying, "There it is, I can see the ridge. You have almost made it my friend, just a little further to go."

Suddenly there was a terrible noise, an angry roaring that was so loud it seemed as though the air around them vibrated.

"What on earth is that?" Ffain asked.

"The lions, they have discovered we are gone," Arthur answered. He turned to Zephyr, "Hurry my friend, you must hurry. Look you are almost there."

Ffain looked up at the ridge; they were so close now he could see Uther's men waving at them, urging them to go faster.

"Please father," Sirocco begged Zephyr. "It's not much further; you've almost made it, just one last push."

Poor Zephyr panted with effort as he tried to make his tired legs move faster over the rough ground. Ffain looked back, he could see the approaching army clearly now, the lion's standard flying over the men's heads in the morning breeze. As he watched he saw two of the leading lions break rank and begin to run swiftly towards the little group as they struggled along.

Ffain turned towards the ridge, they were almost there, he could see the line of fortification and Uther's men peering over, he could hear their voices shouting out encouragements to them. Would they make it? Zephyr's breathing was becoming more and more laboured; he was beginning to slow down again. The two lions were gaining on them steadily, their long, loping strides eating up the distance that separated them. Ffain knew he had to do something.

"Keep him moving, you're almost there!" he shouted out to Arthur and Sirocco, as he spread his mighty wings and flew up into the air.

Maybe it was because of his colour, being green against the grass and trees, but it appeared that it was only now, as he soared into the sky, that the enemy realised that there was a dragon present. Ffain heard a collective gasp of surprise from the approaching army as he rose up and circled back towards them. Several of the lions, and most of the men, hesitated, unwilling to take on the might of a dragon, and the army's forward progress began to falter.

The two lions ahead of them also stopped when they saw Ffain; the leading one lifted his head, tossed back his black mane and emitted a blood curdling roar up into the sky, before continuing the pursuit, the second lion followed. Ffain flew down and skimmed across the ground just in front of Black Mane.

"Turn back, turn back," he called down. "The unicorns are defeated, let them leave in peace."

Black Mane crouched as the dragon flew towards

him, and then sprang into the air with his deadly claws unsheathed. Ffain felt a tug, followed by a sharp pain in his wing, for a moment he was unbalanced, but he managed to correct his flight and circled again towards the lions. Some of the soldiers following cheered the lion on and Ffain heard someone shout, "That'll learn yer, go home yer great lizard!"

Black Mane stopped and watched Ffain approaching, the second lion standing a short distance behind him.

"There is no need for this," Ffain called out. "Too much blood has been spilt, you can stop it now. You have what you want, the Wide World is yours."

"This has nothing to do with you, dragon," Black Mane roared. "You shouldn't even be here. Go back where you came from, back to all the other snivelling, cowardly reptiles."

Ffain was stung by the contempt he heard in the lion's voice, was this really how dragons were remembered in the Wide World? He felt shocked, had his father been right after all? This wasn't his battle; he wasn't wanted here, maybe he should just go and leave them to get on with it. Then a tide of anger swept the shock away. Why not just burn the whole place?

He looked up at the ridge, Arthur, Zephyr and Sirocco had almost reached the top. Some of the men had left the fortress and come out to help the wounded unicorn to safety, putting their own lives at risk. He heard his father's voice in his head reciting the code of chivalry, 'Courage, honour, justice and the readiness to help the weak'. Not all humans were bad, he thought, they deserved the chance to sort out their own world.

Taking advantage of the dragon's distraction, Black Mane bounded forward again, the second lion following more slowly. Ffain could see the group of men gathered around Zephyr as he struggled to get a foothold up onto the ridge. The injured unicorn was hardly visible as Arthur and the soldiers closed ranks around him, their combined effort almost lifting Zephyr up to the safety of the earth wall of the fortress. Regardless of his own safety Sirocco turned to protect them, and faced the charging lion.

Ffain knew he had to act quickly, he flew on and then turned, crossing in front of the rushing lion, as he did so he blew out a long stream of fire and a line of flames blazed across the lion's path.

Black Mane barely hesitated before bunching up his powerful back legs and leaping through the flames to continue his charge. Ffain watched the lion with grudging admiration; you certainly couldn't deny his courage. Sirocco galloped away from the flames in an effort to rejoin his father, who had finally gained the safety of the fortress. Looking back, Arthur saw Black Mane leap through the wall of flame, and shouted out a warning.

Ffain saw Sirocco change direction, lower his head, and prepare to face the lion's onslaught. Black Mane was almost upon him now, too close for Ffain to risk using his fire again. The gap between the charging lion and the galloping unicorn was narrowing by the second; surely the little unicorn would never

survive such a charge. Ffain almost couldn't bear to watch but just as the two were about two meet, and Black Mane was already beginning to lift his huge front paws, claws at the ready; Sirocco swerved to one side, swung swiftly round and caught the lion's hindquarters with a glancing blow of his horn.

The lion stumbled, unbalanced; Ffain seized the opportunity and swooped down towards Black Mane, closer and closer. The lion was readying himself to charge again, Sirocco stood watching him with an eerie calmness, resigned to his fate. The dragon could see the startled looks on the faces of the soldiers lining the wall of the fortress as they felt the rush of air from his wings pass over them. Just as Black Mane began to leap, Ffain reached down and snatched the lion up in his powerful talons, Black Mane gave a roar of anger and surprise, and struggled for freedom as the dragon lifted him into the air, but Ffain merely tightened his grip until Black Mane's body swung limply in the air.

The dragon swiftly covered the distance back to the lion's army that now appeared to be in complete disarray. Most of the men cowered away as Ffain approached; a few of them released their arrows which glanced harmlessly off the dragon's scales. The lions shrank back as Ffain dropped Black Mane's body into their midst, where it landed in an undignified heap. The dragon looked around searching for the lion's standard, knowing the leader of the soldiers would be nearby. He looked down at the man beside it, who returned Ffain's gaze steadily as the dragon spoke.

"Your people deserve better than this," he waved a

paw towards where Black Mane lay, surrounded by his fellow lions. "You should remember; courage, honour, justice and the readiness to help the weak."

The man gave a brief nod of acknowledgement as Ffain turned and flew away back to his friends. The soldiers cheered as he glided over the fortress, he saw King Uther, Arthur and Sirocco standing on top of the small hill, next to the rowan tree that marked the portal.

"Well done, well done," Arthur greeted him, patting Ffain on the back as he landed beside them. "You really have saved the day."

"We owe you a great debt, my friend," said Uther.

"And I, an even greater one," Sirocco smiled up at him. "All the unicorns are safe, including my father, thanks to you."

"No, not just me," Ffain said modestly. "What happened to the other lion?"

"Oh, he soon slunk off when he saw what happened to the first one," Uther said with a chuckle. "And with a few of my men's arrows in his bottom for good luck, but you are bleeding, are you badly hurt?"

Ffain looked down at his wing with some surprise, he had forgotten all about Black Mane clawing him. There was a ragged tear, from which dark, red droplets of blood were dripping onto the ground, where they fell the grass withered away leaving bare soil.

"The curse of the dragon's blood," said Arthur with awe. "I never thought I would see it, nothing will grow here now."

"You must go back and get your wound seen to," said Uther.

"But what about you?" asked Ffain. "Are you safe? Do you think it is over?"

"No," said Uther thoughtfully, looking across towards the fort. "It isn't over, there is still a lot to be resolved; but we humans must make our own world and allow the creatures to return to theirs. Your job is done here, my friend, you and Sirocco must return to your families. Go with our thanks and the knowledge that we will never forget you. This place will remain as a monument to the courage and honour of the dragon and the unicorn."

Edward took a long drink of water to ease his throat, which was dry after so much talking. For a moment Toby and Sox sat in silence still picturing in their heads the scene that Edward had described.

Sox was the first to speak, "So that is why no grass grows on top of Dragon Hill, because my father's blood was spilt here."

Toby looked up at his father eagerly, "And the White Horse, Dad. It isn't a horse at all, is it? It's a unicorn."

Edward smiled at his son, "I knew you'd understand."

"But what happened to King Uther and Arthur?" Toby asked.

"Yes," added Sox. "And what happened to the portal? It's not here now."

Edward cleared his throat and began to explain.

"Nothing happened for a while, but King Uther was right, it wasn't over. The people blamed the unicorns' escape on the lions and they were very angry with them, after a lot of arguing they sent the lions away to live in a distant country.

"King Uther kept his men on in the fort, like soldiers everywhere they passed the time by telling each other stories of battles and bravery. They decided to make the figure of the unicorn on the hillside. They placed it on this side so it faced the portal and they made it so big because, although they knew no dragon would ever be allowed into the Wide World again, they just hoped that if one should ever happen to fly pass, he would recognise it for what it was. Not only a monument in memory of the unicorns but also for the dragons, because who else, apart from the birds, would be able to appreciate that massive figure.

"Once the lions were gone, the people turned their anger on King Uther, who, they thought, had summoned Ffain to help the unicorns. A terrible battle was fought on the hill during which King Uther was killed. Prince Arthur buried his father here, on Dragon Hill, before retreating back to the mountains with his army.

"The victorious army was so angry when they found the monument to the unicorns, their first thought was to destroy it, but the size of it made this a daunting task. It was easier just to cover over the horn so that the figure appeared to be just that of a horse.

"When the entrance to the portal was discovered next to the rowan tree, at the top of this hill, the tree was chopped down, and the top of the hill was removed and levelled to ensure the portal was blocked forever. The humans were so frightened by the thought of any dragon ever returning to the Wide World, the order went out that all rowan trees were to be destroyed just in case, they too, were marking the entrance to a portal.

"Are you ready to climb up to the fort now?" Edward asked Toby, as he packed away the remains of their picnic. "I've got a feeling I know what Sox wants to do."

The little dragon was opening and closing his wings, hopping up and down with impatience, he looked up at Edward.

"I want to fly past, I want to see the unicorn from the air, just as King Uther's men wanted it to be seen by dragons."

"Well, you should be alright," Edward replied, looking around. "I can't see any people; I think they must have all gone home."

Toby and Edward made their way back down the steps from Dragon Hill and crossed the road. They began to climb up the steep path on the opposite hillside, Sox flying beside them; it didn't take long to reach the start of the white figure.

"Here it is," Sox shouted with excitement, as he whirled up into the air. "Whoopee, I'm off!"

Toby stopped and examined the part of the figure beside them.

"It's well made Dad, isn't it?" he said, admiring the skill with which the chalk had been cut and laid in the turf.

"Well, don't forget it has been restored, but yes, I think Uther's men meant it to last a long time."

Toby wished he could fly like Sox, it really was impossible to see the figure clearly from the ground. He and Edward trudged on up the hill in silence, when they reached the top and stopped to catch their breath, Edward pointed ahead saying, "Over there, look, that's the remains of King Uther's fortress."

As they walked across Toby tried to picture how it must have looked to Ffain, all those hundreds of years ago, as he had flown over the hilltop and seen the men digging below him. Edward and Toby climbed up on top of the earth wall and began to walk around the perimeter of the fortress.

"It's much bigger than I thought it would be," said Toby.

"Yes, Uther really believed they would have to stay here for some time, after all he didn't know a dragon was coming to help."

Toby looked around at the windswept fortress and out over the surrounding countryside, that the defeated unicorns had struggled across to safety, led by the valiant Arthur. There was a flash of green and purple and Sox landed beside him with a soft thump.

"Marvellous," he panted. "Absolutely marvellous, I've got so much I want to ask Dad when I get back."

"Yes," Toby agreed. "I've still got a lot I want to ask my Dad too."

He looked up at Edward.

"You still haven't explained how you met Ffain."

"Another day, I promise," Edward replied.

Then seeing the look on his son's face added, "Another day, soon."

Down in the car park, at the foot of White Horse Hill, an elderly man was struggling to lift a heavy picnic basket into the boot of his car.

"Honestly Gwyneth, I don't know why you have to bring so much paraphernalia for, what's supposed to be, just a simple day out."

"Get away with you Owen, I didn't notice you complaining about the amount of food there was, most of which is inside you now, anyway."

Gwyneth stopped talking as something caught her eye.

"What on earth? Look Owen, look up there, by the horse, there's something flying about, whatever is it?"

Owen looked up to where his wife was pointing.

"It must be a bird surely, bit of an odd colour though. It almost looks purple. I think it's too big to be a bird, is it a hang glider?"

"No, too small for that, where are the binoculars?"

"I've got them," said Owen, retrieving the binoculars from the bottom of the picnic basket and lifting them to his eyes. "Blooming hell Gwyneth, I think you'd better take a look at this!"

"Now, now Owen, there's no need for that sort of language," his wife reprimanded him as she took the binoculars. "Good heavens, is that what I think it is?"

She lowered the binoculars and stared at her husband in disbelief; Owen took them from her and focussed again on the green and purple object as it fluttered past the White Horse.

"I don't believe it, it's just not possible and it doesn't make any sense," he said as the thing disappeared over the hill.

"I know they call it Dragon Hill," Gwyneth remarked. "But I thought that was because of Uther Pendragon. We did see it, didn't we? We did both really see it?"

"Yes," said Owen as he shut the boot of the car firmly. "But I don't think we should tell anyone else we did. They'd never believe us; they'd think we've gone mad. Come on, let's get home, back to the mountains, at least you know what's what when you're there."

"Yes, it's been a long day; may be we're just a bit overtired," Gwyneth said as she opened the passenger door of the car and got in.

"Yes, maybe," her husband agreed. He looked down at the car, there was a sticker on the boot, it was a flag, showing a red dragon on a green and white background. Owen gave it a pat as he went to get in the car.

"Dragon Hill, eh?"

ALL THE FUN OF THE FAIR

Toby and Sox were quiet in the car on the way home, each of them wrapped in their own thoughts, thinking back over what they had learnt that day. Toby was the first to speak.

"I've been thinking about dragons; why does the whole Wide World just assume they are not real? If they never existed, then how did they get made up? I mean, why make them up in the first place?"

Toby frowned at the trouble he was having getting his feelings into words.

"Oh, you know what I mean, don't you Dad?"

Edward smiled, but didn't take his eyes off the road.

"Yes, I think I understand what you're getting at. I've always thought it strange that almost every country in the world has some type of dragon figure in its folklore; now, why should that be if dragons weren't here at some point? And another strange thing is that, in most of the other countries dragons are regarded as good creatures. It only seems to be here, in England, that we think of them as bad or evil; but I think we can guess why that is can't we?"

"When I grow up I'm going to write a book all about the history of dragons."

"Good idea son, but I still don't expect anyone will believe it's true. You're very quiet Sox, is everything okay?"

"I've been thinking Mr Edward, about King Uther. You said the people blamed him for my Dad coming. Do you think he might not have been killed if my Dad hadn't come?"

The little dragon sounded very worried.

Edward sighed, "Well, that's a tricky one Sox, and we have no way of ever finding out the truth. One thing I do know, most of the unicorns would not have survived if Ffain hadn't come. They would never have left Zephyr behind, all of them, including Sirocco, would probably have perished. Imagine what the Inner World would be like without the unicorns."

"Hmph," Sox snorted. "Well, it would certainly be a lot quieter without Swift charging around."

"And," Edward continued. "King Uther and Prince

Arthur may well have both been killed if they had been forced to defend the fortress against the lions. At least Ffain made the people realise what vain and foolish creatures the lions were."

Toby and Sox fell silent again as they thought all this through. They were almost home when they noticed that a fun fair had set up on the edge of town.

"What's a fun fair?" asked Sox. "It sounds like somewhere you go to buy fun."

"Well, I suppose that's what it is really," replied Edward. "There are all sorts of rides you can go on and stalls where you try to win prizes by shooting or throwing things. Its Saturday tomorrow, would you like to go? When are your parents expecting you back?"

"It sounds very strange," said Sox. "I would like to go and have a look, and my Mum and Dad know I'm with Toby so they won't be worried."

"That's settled then, we'll go tomorrow evening, fun fairs always look better at night, when the lights are on."

"Great!" said Toby. "And I've just remembered something else too, Mum's strawberry jam. We'll be able to have some for lunch tomorrow. You'll love it Sox, it's absolutely delicious, even better than the jam the nippies make."

The following morning Toby asked Sally if they could make some scones to have with the strawberry jam at lunch time. Toby liked helping his mother to bake things, there was something very satisfying in mixing ingredients in a bowl, putting them in the oven and then eating the delicious cakes or biscuits that resulted.

Today he brought Sox down and placed him in a

corner where he wouldn't be in the way, but would be able to see what was taking place. Sally raised her eyebrows when she saw him putting the dragon on the kitchen worktop, but didn't say anything. She helped Toby as he carefully measured out and mixed the ingredients for the scones, and she made sure he didn't roll the mixture out too thinly before cutting it into rounds. Once the scones were in the oven, and the timer was set, Sally asked Toby to go and find his father, who was working in the garden, and tell him that it was time for coffee.

As soon as Toby had gone out of the door Sally crossed over to where Sox was sitting. The little dragon didn't move as she leant forwards and examined him very closely. Sox held his breath, fixed his eyes on a point over Sally's shoulder and tried not to blink; her face was just inches away from his. Sally slowly put out her hand and ran a finger gently down Sox's front. It didn't feel like a cuddly toy, she thought. She used two fingers this time, and ran them across the little dragon's tummy more firmly. She thought she felt a small vibration, then suddenly Sox, who was unable to contain himself any longer, snorted with laughter and a puff of smoke rose up from his nostrils and into the air. Sally screamed and jumped back with fright just as Toby and Edward came in through the back door.

"What's going on? What's happened?" asked Edward with concern, as he put his arm around his wife's shoulders.

Sally pushed him away and pointed at Sox with a trembling finger.

"What's going on? You tell me what's going on, that **THING**, whatever it is, is alive!"

Sox looked at Edward.

"Sorry," he said with a shrug. "I couldn't help it, she tickled me."

"And, it speaks!" Sally almost screamed at them.

"It's alright Mum," said Toby. "It's only Sox, he's a dragon and he's my friend. He lives in the Inner World and he comes to see me sometimes."

"A dragon? Stop talking nonsense Toby, you know perfectly well there's no such things as dragons. It must be some sort of lizard that's escaped from somewhere."

"Sally, Sally," said Edward, trying again to put his arm round his wife's shoulders. "Please calm down, we can explain everything."

Sally looked up at her husband with shock.

"We? What do you mean, we? Do you mean to say you know about this…this…creature."

"Look," said Edward. "Why don't we sit down and have a cup of coffee. Then Toby, Sox and I can explain everything to you."

He held up a hand as he saw Sally was about to speak again.

"I know, I know, we should have told you weeks ago, and I'm very sorry that we had to keep it a secret from you. I hated having to deceive you."

"Weeks ago! Honestly Edward, how long has this been going on?"

"Well, years actually," said Edward, looking rather embarrassed as he switched on the kettle and took the coffee cups out of the cupboard. "Hundreds and hundreds of years, and I'm afraid it is going to take quite some time to explain it all to you."

He was interrupted by the beeping of the oven timer.

"I've got a feeling we might be very glad of those scones and some of your delicious jam," he said as Sally removed the tray from the oven and placed it on the cooling rack.

"Now, sit down and we'll begin. First of all we have to introduce you to Sox, short for Socrates."

Sox gave a little bow.

"He *is* a dragon and he is the son of a very old friend of mine."

By the time they had finished telling Sally all about the Inner World and the history of the dragons, the scones and jam were finished and the afternoon was almost over. They had explained about Stonehenge, the Vale of the White Horse and how Sox had suddenly appeared in Toby's room.

"Goodness," she remarked. "To think we took him shopping, and into Smithsons too!"

Sally insisted that they went up to Toby's room and looked

under the bed. The three of them lay on the floor with their heads and shoulders under the

bed. Edward was the first to wriggle forward and reach out into the corner.

"You can feel something," he said to Sally. "There's a slight draught coming from the opening, but I'm afraid I'm far too big get through these days.

"I'm surprised you and Sox can get through," Sally said to Toby.

"It is a bit of a squeeze," Toby admitted. "Quite uncomfortable actually, a bit like being sucked up in a vacuum cleaner. Sox seems to shrink somehow when he comes through, he's much bigger in the Inner World, almost as tall as me."

"Well, from what you've told me, a fully grown dragon certainly wouldn't fit through there."

Toby and Sox exchanged a glance, neither of them wanted to even think about the fact that one day they would both be too big to go through the tunnel.

"Let me see," said Sally.

She edged forward and stretched out her hand to feel the corner.

"Oh," she said with disappointment. "I can't feel anything, nothing at all, just walls and floor."

"Maybe, it's because you're an adult," suggested Edward, sitting up. "Perhaps you have to discover it as a child; perhaps it's something to do with children being open minded, you know, prepared to believe things. You do believe us, don't you?"

"Of course I do," Sally answered. "Obviously there is still a lot I don't understand; but how could I not believe you with Sox sitting there. I want to hear what happened with you and Ffain, and about Toby and Sox."

"We still haven't heard about Dad's adventure," Toby pointed out.

Sox nodded in agreement as Edward rose stiffly to his feet and stretched.

"Look, we've been sitting and talking for hours and I promised these two a trip to the fun fair. Why don't we all go, we could do with the fresh air. Tomorrow is Sunday; we've got all day with nothing important to do. I promise I will tell all three of you my story then and after that Toby and Sox can relate their adventure, at least that way you will get to hear everything in the right order."

"You're right," said Sally, getting to her feet. "It's a lot to take in all at once, especially finding out you've got a dragon in the family."

She smiled at Sox. "The fun fair sounds a great idea."

Toby, Edward and Sox were very relieved that Sally knew their secret, they hadn't felt comfortable hiding things from her, life would be a lot easier now. The four of them set off to walk to the fun fair, Sox in his usual place, in Toby's rucksack. Sally was still trying to understand everything they had told her.

"And unicorns as well." Toby heard her remark to Edward. "Now that is hard to believe."

Sox was overwhelmed by the sights and sounds of the fairground. Toby had to warn him several times about wriggling around so much.

"Be careful, someone will see you moving. Just sit still and I'll walk round slowly so you can have a good look."

"Goodness," came Sox's voice from over his shoulder. "What on earth is that? It looks like a cloud

on a stick. Over there, look. Oh my goodness, that child is eating a cloud on a stick!"

Toby looked in the direction that Sox was pointing.

"Oh, it's candy floss; I see what you mean though. I'll get some for you to try if you like, you'll love it."

Sox was entranced by the man catching the wisps of candy floss in his machine and whisking them up onto a stick. Sally and Edward stood either side of Toby, shielding the little dragon from view, as he tried the sticky substance.

"Oh yummy, that's good," Sox smacked his lips in appreciation. "Plum would love this, what a shame I can't take her some back."

"Who is Plum?" asked Sally. "Another dragon?"

"No Mum, she's a fairy," Toby replied.

"A fairy! Now you've got to be pulling my leg."

"It's true, honestly. I'll explain later. Have you had enough Sox? I want to take you on the helter skelter, I think you'll like that."

Fortunately there wasn't a queue, just the man in charge, who was picking at his fingernails in boredom, and a lady, with a toddler in a pushchair. She was standing at the bottom of the slide and calling up to an unseen person in an exasperated manner.

"Oh, come on Belinda. I'm sick to death of waiting. Yer really shouldn't have gone up there if yer was too scared to slide down. Either go for it or come back down the stairs. One more minute and I'm going without yer."

She glanced over at Edward, Sally and Toby.

"Bloomin' kids, I've 'ad it up to 'ere with them," she said, to no one in particular.

Toby picked up a mat from the top of the pile as Edward paid the man in charge. He was just about to start climbing the stairs when the man stopped him.

"Just a minute," said the helter skelter man, barring Toby's way with a hairy arm. "Why don't you leave your rucksack with your Dad? That would be safer and a lot easier than carrying it all the way up the stairs."

Edward helped Toby off with the rucksack; Toby lifted Sox out and carried him over to the stairs.

"Aw, taking your little friend with you for the ride, are you?" said the man. "That's nice."

Toby felt Sox about to protest, he gripped him a little harder and began to climb the steep spiral staircase inside the helter skelter.

"Little friend, indeed," the dragon said with scorn

as soon as they were out of earshot. "Honestly, some people."

"Ssh," warned Toby. "We're nearly at the top."

They found the exit blocked by a small girl, who, Toby assumed, must be Belinda. She was sitting on her mat at the top of the slide, holding on so tightly to either side, her knuckles were white.

"Are you alright?" Toby asked.

"I'm too scared to let go," she replied tearfully. "It's too high, I'm frightened."

Sox lifted up his head and gave her a big, toothy dragon smile.

"I'm sure it's quite safe," he said kindly.

Belinda looked at the dragon with horror, lifted both her hands to her mouth in surprise, and promptly disappeared from view. The sound of her screams came floating back up to them above the background noise of the fun fair.

"I don't think you should have done that," Toby remarked.

But Sox wasn't listening, he was too busy staring all around taking in the aerial view of the fairground; looking at all the stalls and rides laid out below them in a mass of blazing coloured lights.

"Oh Toby, it's wonderful," he said, turning his head from side to side.

"It's great, isn't it," Toby agreed, settling himself on the mat with Sox grasped firmly on his knee. "But this is the best bit."

He pushed off from the top of the helter skelter and they slipped forward gathering speed as they slid round and down, the coloured lights flashing past faster and faster.

"Whee!" Sox shouted with glee.

But it was over all too soon and they bumped to a halt as Edward caught them at the bottom.

"Whatever was the matter with that little girl?" asked Sally. "She seemed very upset."

"I don't really know Mum, I think she was just a bit frightened. Can we go to the bumper cars now?" Toby asked quickly, before Sally could ask him anything else.

"Okay," said Edward. "And after that let's go and get a hot dog, I'm starving."

"Why would your father want a dog that's hot?" asked Sox in Toby's ear as they walked over to the dodgems.

"Oh Sox," Toby laughed. "It's not a hot dog; it's a type of sausage in a bread roll. It's just called a hot dog."

"I don't think I'll ever understand what you humans eat," said Sox, with a shake of his head. "Clouds on sticks, dogs in rolls, but I must say your Mum's jam and scones were delicious. What's this we're going on now?"

"Ssh," Toby warned him, as he placed the rucksack on the seat next to him in the bumper car.

As he leaned over and fastened the seat belt around the bag so it wouldn't topple over, he whispered, "They're called bumper cars, but the idea is to try and miss everyone else, not to hit them. They're also called dodgems, and that's what we're going to try to do."

A siren sounded and the dodgems began to move, Toby started off slowly and then began to go a little faster as he gained confidence. A car, driven by a small boy seated beside his father, banged into them.

"Sorry," the man said, and the little boy grinned at Toby.

"That's alright," Toby replied, smiling back.

He turned the steering wheel heading to the back of the ride where there was more room.

He heard someone call out, "There he is, let's get 'im!"

A dodgem banged violently into the back of them, the impact threw Toby's head back with a jerk, hurting his neck. He looked back over his shoulder and saw a teenage boy laughing at him from the car behind.

"Watch out," said Toby. "You're not supposed to… Ow"

He didn't get to finish his sentence as another dodgem, also driven by a teenage boy, rammed into him at the front making him bite his tongue. The two boys laughed at him, Toby didn't know whether to feel cross or afraid. He turned the steering wheel of his car and tried to drive off but the boy at the front pulled up beside him blocking the way.

"Whatcha think you're playing at then, frightening my little sister? Not so funny now, is it?" the boy sneered at him.

"What do you mean?" Toby asked in confusion. "I didn't…oh, do you mean the little girl on the helter skelter?"

While Toby had been talking the boy behind had got out of his dodgem and walked round beside Toby, now he leant over him threateningly.

"Watcha want me to do to 'im, Gav? Shall I give 'im a smack?"

Toby looked around to try and spot his parents, they were nowhere to be seen, and the man who was supposed to be in charge of the bumper cars was far away, on the other side of the ride, talking to some girls.

"Not so brave now, are ya?" Gavin smirked. "'Ere, what's that in 'is bag Danny?"

"No, don't!"

Toby tried to get hold of the rucksack, but he was too slow. Gavin had a painful grip on his arm and Toby watched helplessly as Danny pulled Sox out of the bag.

"Aw, look. Has diddums got a cuddly toy, then? It

don't feel very cuddly, blimey it's ugly! What's it meant to be?"

"Chuck it over, Danny."

"No!" Toby shouted.

"Ow!" Danny dropped Sox to the floor. "Blimey there's something sharp, felt like it bit me!"

He drew back his leg to give the dragon a kick.

"I wouldn't do that, if I were you," said a stern voice.

All three of them looked round to see Edward and the dodgems man standing behind them.

"And," Edward continued. "You can let go of my son's arm."

Gavin dropped Toby's arm, the boy jumped out of the car and went across to pick up Sox from where he lay beside Danny.

"I know you two," the dodgems man was saying. "You've caused trouble on the fairground before. I think you'd better clear off before I call the police."

Danny gave a sudden yelp of pain and began to hop about.

"Help Gav, 'elp! Somefings 'ot, it's burning me."

There was a wisp of smoke coming from Danny's ankle.

"Blimey Danny, yer jeans is on fire! 'Ow did that 'appen?"

"Stop wasting my time," the dodgems man was beginning to sound very angry. "Go on, clear off out of it! You're costing me money."

Danny jumped down from the ride, sat down on the ground and started hitting his ankle with his hands.

The dodgems man gave Gavin a shove in the back and sent him sprawling on top of his friend.

"Come on Toby," said Edward with a smile, as he picked up the rucksack. "Let's go and get that hot dog, the smell of cooking is making me even hungrier."

They made their way over to Sally, who was holding three large hot dogs oozing with onions and ketchup.

"What was that all about?" she asked. "Are you alright Toby?"

"I'm fine," he assured her, taking one of the hot dogs.

"Yes, everything's okay," said Edward. "I think we can add another one to the list of dragon believers, don't you Sox?"

Sox looked up as Edward reached across for his hot dog and a dollop of ketchup landed on the dragon's nose.

"Oh dear Mr Edward, I think your dog is bleeding. Fun fairs certainly are strange places, aren't they?"

Toby, Edward and Sally exploded with laughter, Edward started choking on a piece of bread and Sally had to thump him on the back.

"Oh Sox," she said, blinking tears of laughter from her eyes. "You really are priceless."

The little dragon looked at them all in astonishment.

"Humans, I'll never understand them."

After their encounter with Gavin and Danny, Toby and Sox decided to opt for something a little less exciting. There was a beautifully restored old merry-go-round, Sox was fascinated by the painted wooden horses going up and down, round and round, whilst the organ at the centre of the ride piped its tunes. Toby, Edward and Sally chose a horse each and climbed on board.

"Ooh, I like this," Sox whispered in Toby's ear, from the rucksack, as their horse carried them round, rising and falling gently. "It's almost like flying."

"I think flying with your Dad is a lot more exciting than this," Toby replied, remembering the thrill of sitting on Ffain's back with the wind blowing into his face and the earth rushing past beneath them.

When the merry-go-round finished they wandered round the stalls. Toby and Edward each had a turn on the rifle range, but neither of them managed to win a prize.

"Just as well," said Sally, looking at the array of cheap, cuddly toys on offer. "What on earth would we have done with it?"

"I almost got one," said Toby. "But every time I aimed the rifle Sox kept saying, 'Now, shoot now' right in my ear, and it was very off putting."

"Sorry," said Sox. "I was just trying to help."

"How about the hoop-la?"

Edward suggested as they walked past the stall.

"No, the rings never fit over the prizes, and I don't want a coconut." Toby added, as the man in charge of the shy held out a handful of wooden balls.

"Five throws for a pound."

"Well, I'll have a go," said Edward. "We can always hang it in the garden for the birds."

Edward's second shot moved a coconut in its cup, and with his final ball he managed to dislodge it completely.

"Well done Dad."

"It's the biggest nut I have ever seen," said Sox.

"It's got juice inside you can drink,"

Edward shook the coconut near Sox's head, so he could hear the liquid sloshing around.

"It's very nice; you can try it when we get home. Now, what else is there?"

He looked around.

"How about the hall of mirrors? You'll like this one, Sox."

Edward paid the entrance fee and they went in.

"My goodness, that is the strangest thing I have ever seen," said Sox, as he looked in a mirror over Toby's shoulder.

 The boy appeared to have very long, thin legs, almost no body at all, and two large heads, one human and the other a dragon.

"Oh dear," laughed Sally at her extremely wide reflection. "I don't think I should have eaten that hot dog."

They walked through the hall slowly, laughing at

their distorted reflections in the mirrors and trying out various silly poses to make the effects even more exaggerated.

"Silly, but fun," said Edward, as they emerged from the exit. "Is everyone ready to go home now?"

They all agreed they were ready and they began to make their way back to the house.

"I can't wait to hear the rest of your stories," said Sally as they walked through the quiet streets.

"Me too," agreed Sox.

"Dad, I've wanted to ask you about the name of our house. How did it get to be called 'Rowans', and why are all the rowan trees there? Is it because of the tunnel?"

"Yes, you must remember it was hundreds of years ago that the rowan trees were ordered to be destroyed. So long ago, everyone forgot secret portals, and dragons became mythical creatures that you told stories about to frighten your children. The trees survived in the mountains and remote areas and gradually they began to reappear elsewhere. When I discovered the portal at our house and learnt about the trees' significance for the Inner World, I was determined to mark it in some

way. I think I wanted to make up for the

destruction that took place on Dragon Hill, and I wanted to mark the place just in case a dragon should ever pass by."

Edward smiled at Sox.

"I had to wait until I was older and I had my first job. I saved up and one Christmas I gave the trees to my parents as a gift, and I made the sign saying 'Rowans' to hang on the gate. They just thought it was a nice present, up until then the house had just had a number. I took advantage of my parents being away one weekend, just before Christmas, and planted the trees myself. My Dad could never understand why I hadn't planted them in a circle or a nice straight line."

Edward smiled at the puzzled looks on Sally and Toby's faces; he knew they were both thinking of the six trees in their garden.

"It's a sort of cross, isn't it?" asked Sally.

"No, have you ever thought what they would look like if you saw them from the air?"

"Oh, I get it," said Toby. "It's not a cross; it's an arrow, isn't it? And, it points to my bedroom."

"Oh, my word, you're right Toby, so it does!" his mother exclaimed in surprise. "I never realised before."

"But what about the rowan trees in the Inner World?" asked Sox. "There is something special about them, isn't there? Mistral sent a message to my mother to remember the rowan tree, what was that all about?"

They had reached the gate to the house; Edward held it open for Toby and Sally to pass through.

"That's your mother's story, I promised I would tell you tomorrow and I will. But first I must finish Ffain's story and tell you what happened to him when he went back home."

And so he did.

PART 3 THE HOMECOMING

Ffain's return to the Inner World was greeted with mixed emotions; to the unicorns, the hares and all the other creatures of the Inner World he was a hero, but as far as the dragons were concerned he was an oath breaker.

He went to the sanctuary and Lavender tried to explain her feelings to him as she tended to the tear in his wing.

"It's not that I'm not pleased that the unicorns have

been rescued, of course I am. Lochinvar tried to persuade them to join us here months ago. And, it's not that I don't appreciate your courage and resolution, but your father swore a solemn oath that none of us would return to the Wide World, and you have broken that promise; and for a dragon to break his word – well, I don't think it has ever been heard of before. Goodness knows what your father will make of it all."

Ffain was dreading seeing his parents, especially Lochinvar, but he knew he couldn't put it off any longer. After making sure that Zephyr was comfortably settled, he began to say goodbye to Sirocco.

"I have to go now; my parents are, um ..., they are...expecting me. I'm sure your father will be fine now, Lavender will take good care of him."

Sirocco heard the reluctance to leave in the dragon's voice.

"Is it far, the place where you live?"

"I live on the High Mountain, it's not too far as the dragon flies."

Ffain gave a sigh as he thought about life back in his parent's castle after all the excitement of the last two days. Sirocco seemed to read his thoughts.

"It's going to be hard to adjust, isn't it? To get back to normal after the fury of the battlefield, but it's better to live in peace, I think."

Ffain regarded the young unicorn for a long moment and thought about all Sirocco had been through, the fear and dread of battling against a force you knew was superior to your own, the trauma of seeing his father so very nearly killed and the bravery he had shown risking his own life to save others; the dragon sighed again.

Seeing his despondency Sirocco tried to cheer him up.

"At least you go home with the knowledge that you have done a great service to the unicorns, we will be forever in your debt, Ffain the Lion Slayer."

Ffain gave a snort of amusement.

"Well, I suppose that's better than Ffain the Oath Breaker."

Sirocco looked at the dragon with concern.

"You seem very troubled my friend, would it help to tell someone your worries?"

After all they had been through together Ffain knew that he could trust the young unicorn completely; suddenly he had an overwhelming desire to confess, to tell someone what he had done and try to lessen the burden he felt by sharing it. He led Sirocco away to a quiet spot where they wouldn't be overheard and told him the whole story. He described how he had begged Lochinvar to let him go into the Wide World and his father's refusal to break his oath. How, in desperation, he had gone to find Lucifer and the terrible vow the yellow dragon had forced Ffain to make.

"I had to do it, I just had to. I knew the unicorns needed help, after all it's what dragons do; or used to do," he added bitterly. "And now I have to go home and face my father, he is going to be furious. I only hope he never learns about my promise to Lucifer, 'the Oath of the White Dragon', ha! He would probably kill me himself!"

"But surely when he hears of your great courage

and what you achieved, he will not be so angry?" asked Sirocco.

"I wish I could believe that, still I suppose I can't put it off any longer, I'd better go home and face the music. Thank you for listening to me, it has been a great help to be able to share this with someone, you really are a true friend."

"Go well, and be assured; your secret is safe with me. You know where to find me if ever you should need to do so."

Ffain began to make his way out of the healing sanctuary towards the space that the dragons used for taking off and landing, he was nearly there when a movement caught the corner of his eye. He turned to see Lavender and Horatio's daughter, Petunia, hesitating at the edge of the clearing.

"Oh, it's you Tunie. Do you want something?"

The small purple dragon looked up at him nervously.

"I um…, I just …um, wanted to say."

"Oh for goodness sake, will you just spit it out," said Ffain impatiently. "I know what you're thinking, your mother made that quite clear. Actually no, I don't need to hear it all again from you, so you needn't bother. I'll just go home and hear it all again from my parents, shall I?" He spread his wings in preparation for flying.

"N-no," Petunia blurted out. "You don't understand, I think what you did was wonderful. I've heard what the unicorns are calling you, Ffain the Lion Slayer, you must be very brave." She stared up at him with adoration in her green eyes.

Ffain squirmed with embarrassment, the admiration he saw in Petunia's face made him feel very uncomfortable. She would probably despise me if she knew the truth, he thought and this made him feel angry and, even though he knew in his heart it wasn't fair or rational, he rounded on Petunia.

"Well that makes everything alright then, doesn't it?" he said sarcastically. "As long as little Miss Petunia thinks I'm brave, everything will be fine."

Petunia gave a gasp, and took a step back as if he had struck her. Ffain could see her eyes beginning to fill with tears and he knew his behaviour had been totally unacceptable. He wanted to apologise, he wanted to put his paws around Petunia and comfort her. He may have been angry with the other dragons, but he was furious with himself. He looked at the purple dragon's grief stricken face and Ffain the great warrior melted away, instead he felt like the biggest coward in the world. He cautiously reached out a paw towards Petunia but she shrank away from him. With his emotions in turmoil Ffain spread his wings and flew off without saying another word.

Petunia slumped to the ground in misery, what had she done? You are so stupid, she admonished herself, and now Ffain thinks you're an idiot too, just like everyone else does, and maybe they're right, you are an idiot. She gave a sob of self-pity and a large tear rolled down her nose.

"Ahem, Miss Petunia, are you alright?"

Petunia looked at the nippy who had suddenly materialised beside her.

"No, not really Chalky," she replied, and then, much to the hare's surprise, she asked. "Do you think I'm an idiot?"

"No, of course not," said Chalky looking startled. "Why, you're the daughter of Lavender and Horatio, two of the cleverest dragons in the Inner World."

"So you're saying, because my parents are clever, I must be too. I don't think that's how it works. If that were the case Aralu would be bad because his father is Lucifer."

"But being clever isn't everything; you're one of the kindest, caring dragons I know, and the prettiest."

"Really Chalky?" asked Petunia brightening up. "Do you really think I'm pretty?"

"Yes definitely, trust me; I know a pretty face when I see one."

"Thank you Chalky, you're very kind. Did you want something?"

"Yes, your mother's looking for you; she wants to know where you put the willow bark. She says, it's not in its usual place, and she can't find it anywhere."

"Goodness, I forgot. I was tidying up and I thought I would try a new organising system, but I'm not sure now I can remember how it worked."

Petunia chewed absentmindedly on a claw as she tried to recall where she had put the willow bark.

"Perhaps you'll remember if you come back to the treatment area," Chalky suggested. "I expect your mother could do with some help."

"Of course, I'll come straightaway."

The hare and the dragon set off down the path together.

"Now, how did it go again? Was I placing them by size or by colour? I know I thought the shelves of medicines looked much prettier at the time."

"Yes, Miss Petunia," the hare said in an exasperated voice. "I'm sure they did."

Ffain flew slowly up the river valley; he looked up at the High Mountain far above him, its summit wreathed in dark clouds. He knew the weather there always reflected the mood of its master; he really was not in a hurry to get home. A movement and a flash of yellow in the foothills below him caught his eye, and he circled downwards, preparing to land.

"What do you want?" Aralu asked suspiciously as Ffain approached him.

"Just wondering how you were," Ffain replied.

"Huh, since when have you been bothered how I am? Anyway, I hear you're the great hero these days, why on earth should the mighty lion slayer be bothered with an ordinary dragon like me."

"Oh no," groaned Ffain. "Not you as well, how did you…no, don't tell me, I can guess, the rainbow mice, right?"

Aralu nodded and Ffain shook his head in astonishment. "They have got to be the fastest form of communication, ever known."

"So why are you here Ffain? Come to show off, have you?"

Ffain looked at Aralu in disbelief.

"Why are you being like this? Can't I just come, for no reason? We used to be friends, we used to have fun together, until you decided to come back here and mooch about on your own."

Ffain made a sweeping gesture with his paw, indicating the cave they were standing in front of and the surrounding area. It really is a miserable place, he thought, no home comforts at all. Why would anyone rather be here than in the Valley of Jewels or on the High Mountain?

"You just don't understand, do you?" Aralu replied bitterly. "Have you ever thought – have you ever given one moment's thought as to how it feels to always be the odd one out? To watch you, and Petunia, and Magenta, playing happy families with your parents and to not belong; to  always be the extra one, the afterthought, 'Oh, we'd  better include Aralu'," Aralu mimicked. "'Would you like to come too, Aralu dear?' All of you being so kind, so condescending, feeling sorry for me, poor little orphan. Bah! I'm better off on my own."

Ffain was taken aback by the venom in Aralu's voice. It was true, he thought guiltily, he had never imagined what it must have been like for the yellow dragon; even though he and his father hadn't been seeing eye to eye recently the thought of Lochinvar not being around was difficult to imagine, and as for losing Phaedre, his mother, that just didn't bear thinking about. To have had to grow up without either of them to teach him, to guide him, to just have fun with, would have been unbearable.

Aralu continued his tirade, the resentment still obvious in his voice.

"And why am I on my own? Because *they* decided, your blasted father and all the rest of them sent my father away; thought it was the best thing to do. Nasty, evil Lucifer, better not let him have anything to do with his son, he's made the humans hate us and caused our banishment. Well, who cares Ffain? Who cares? The damn humans didn't want us anyway, they killed my mother. Can you blame my father, Ffain? Answer me honestly, can you? Wouldn't you have done the same thing?"

Ffain felt a confusing rush of emotions, he remembered how he had felt on the battlefield when Black Mane and his followers had insulted him. Oh yes, he had wanted to kill then. He remembered King Uther, Prince Arthur and their brave soldiers who had been willing to risk their own lives to save the unicorns, not all humans were bad. He remembered how angry he had been with Lochinvar and then he remembered Lucifer.

"I saw him," he blurted out. "I saw your father. I talked to him, about you."

Aralu stared at the green dragon in astonishment.

"You? You spoke to my father, when … how?"

"I-I had to go to the Back of Beyond for some

ingredients for Lavender, she'd run out, and I, um …, I bumped into him." Ffain finished lamely.

"Is he alright? What did he say?" Aralu asked eagerly.

"He…he asked after you, hoped you were alright, and...and…"

"Yes?" Aralu looked at Ffain with such hope in his eyes; the green dragon knew what he had to say.

"He said to tell you he loves you."

"Oh," Aralu said softly.

Turning slightly away from Ffain, he repeatedly quietly, "He loves me."

The young yellow dragon felt a warm glow inside his chest, my father sent his love; he loves me. He hugged the thought to himself, as if it were the most precious jewel in the world.

"Are you alright?" Ffain asked concerned by the effect his words had caused.

Aralu looked at him, his eyes bright with unshed tears.

"I'm fine thank you, Ffain. And I'm sorry about what I said earlier, it's just that...well, sometimes it's hard, you know?"

"It's okay, I understand, or at least I understand more now," he said with a rueful smile. "Look, I'm going to have to go, my parents will know I'm back by now, and they'll be wondering where I've got to. But I promise I'll come and see  you again soon, or why don't you come to see me? Oh, on second thoughts, maybe that's not such a good idea. I'm not exactly in my Dad's good books at the moment; there will probably be a bit of an atmosphere."

Ffain nodded towards the black clouds hovering over the High Mountain.

"If you know what I mean?"

"The Oath?" asked Aralu.

"Yes."

An awkward silence fell between them as the mention of the oath that Ffain had broken brought back the subject of Lucifer to both their minds.

"Well, I'd better go," Ffain said at last.

"Yes," Aralu agreed. "Thank you for coming Ffain, and thank you for the message. I really appreciate it."

Ffain flew on up the mountain, lost in thought. Poor Aralu, what a miserable life he had. He really did spend far too much time on his own, no wonder he was becoming so short tempered. I will have to go and visit him more often, perhaps on my next trip to see the unicorns. Thinking about going down to the valley again reminded Ffain of his encounter with Petunia. What had that been all about? He still felt embarrassed by his behaviour and didn't understand why he had acted the way he had. She made him feel…she made him feel… How did she make him feel? Peculiar, that was the only way he could think to describe it, she made him feel peculiar. She was awfully pretty though. I wonder if she would like to come with me to visit Aralu. The idea of an outing with Petunia gave him a warm feeling inside, which lasted until he landed in the courtyard of his father's castle, and heard Lochinvar shouting from the great hall.

"And about time too, your mother has been waiting all day. Do you never think about anyone but yourself?"

"Hello Father, yes it's very nice to see you too," Ffain greeted his parent as he entered the room. He went over to Phaedre and gave her a hug.

"Hello Mother, I'm sorry if I have kept you waiting."

Phaedre returned her son's hug warmly and then looked him over with an anxious eye. "Are you alright? You've been hurt," she said noticing the wound on his wing.

She looked up at his face; Ffain could see all the pain and worry he had caused reflected in her eyes.

"Oh Ffain, how could you? Whatever were you thinking of?"

Ffain took a step back and addressed his parents.

"I'm very sorry for the distress I have caused you, but I have to be honest and say that I'm not sorry I went and, if necessary, I would go again."

Phaedre gasped with shock at his words, Ffain lowered his head and prepared himself for the onslaught he expected from his father. There was a moment's silence, then he felt Lochinvar's paw on his shoulder and he looked up to see his father regarding him gravely.

"It is a very difficult thing to be a parent; it's a job that no one can prepare you for, as I expect you may find out one day. Children fill you with joy and despair, and I'm sorry to say it is the latter you have been giving to your mother and me over the past few days.

"You may regard your recent behaviour as being brave and heroic and, in some ways maybe it was, but you have also been deceitful and disobedient, you have lied, you have gone against my orders and above all you have broken an oath. Tell me Ffain, what am I to do with you?"

Ffain looked into his father's face and saw the suffering and pain he had caused; he wished Lochinvar would shout at him. He wanted him to rant and rave in his usual manner, hit him even, anything but this terrible, quiet disappointment.

There was a lump in his throat and he had to swallow hard before replying quietly, "I don't know, Sir."

"No, neither do I son, neither do I," Lochinvar shook his head slowly from side to side with resignation. "However, if what I hear from Sable is true, you are a true warrior."

Ffain glanced up at father in surprise.

"Oh yes, I have heard the whole story but there is

more to being a green dragon than just showing courage
in the heat of battle. Your task now is to prove to your
mother and me, and to the rest of the dragons of the
Inner World that, when my time is over, you will be a
worthy ruler of the High Mountain. Do you think you
are up to the task?"

"I don't know father," Ffain said humbly. "I hope
so."

"I hope so too, Ffain," replied Lochinvar. "I hope so
too, because that is what you are going to do. You are
going to learn all there is to know about the running of
this castle, the guarding of the pass and the duties that
being the ruler of this kingdom entails. And, not only
are you going to learn about all these jobs and tasks
you are going to carry them out, each and every one in
turn, from sweeping the floors, to baking the bread,
from sentry duty, to training the nippies, and when
you have done them all, you will do them all again,
until I am satisfied that you understand all the

responsibilities of being a green dragon. Do you understand?"

"Yes Father."

And that is why no one heard from, or saw anything of, Ffain the Lion Slayer for years, and years, and years.

"But what about you Dad?" asked Toby. "You still haven't told us how you discovered the Inner World."

"Well, hundreds and hundreds of human years passed before that happened, and this really *is* your mother's story, Sox. I'm sorry it has taken me so long to get round to it." Edward smiled at the young dragon. "It all started one day when she was daydreaming as usual, I'm afraid ..."

PART 1. A FELLOW ADVENTURER

VI

"Petunia, Petunia. Where are you?"

The sound of her mother's voice brought the young purple dragon back to the present with a start. Goodness, how long had she been? How much time had passed since Lavender had sent her to find her father's walking stick. Too much, judging by the sound of growing irritation she could hear in her mother's voice as it drew closer to where she sat at the back of their cave in her parent's sleeping quarters.

"There you are," Lavender greeted her in exasperation. "I might have known, wasting time again, off in another one of your daydreams, I expect. I might as well have come to get it myself in the first place. Really, you are useless sometimes, quite useless. Well, did you find your father's stick?"

"I'm so sorry Mama. I did find it, look here it is. It's just that I came across one of Papa's journals from one of your expeditions, and I'm afraid I started to read it. I didn't realise how much time had passed, I only meant to take a quick look, but it was so interesting. All about your trip to Africa and how you discovered the soapweed that you brought back with you. Wasn't it on that same trip that Papa found Neville? It must have been very exciting."

"And meanwhile, whilst you are enjoying your mental trip around the Wide World, your poor father is stuck down in the treatment area unable to move for want of his walking stick. Really Petunia, you are the limit."

"I am sorry Mama, truly. I didn't mean to be so long, please don't be cross. I'll take the stick down to father now, I'll run all the way, it will only take a minute."

Lavender looked down at her daughter's anxious face and felt her anger melt away.

"No, it's alright, we can walk back together. It won't do Horatio any harm to rest that leg for a little longer, and I have got to get back to see to my other patients. One of the nippies has a badly sprained paw and there seems to be a bit of a stomach upset going around. Come along, we can talk on the way."

The two purple dragons set off together following the well-worn path that led from their cave to the healing sanctuary.

"I'm sorry I was cross with you my dear," Lavender said. "But you were rather a long time and your father was growing impatient. I've just changed the dressing on that nasty ulcer he has on his leg. I do wish he would rest it, but he insists on seeing to his plants, even though he knows the nippies are quite capable of tending to them without him being there. At least he has agreed to use the stick and try to put as little weight on his leg as possible. I'm so worried about him, Petunia, that leg isn't healing as it should. If only we had some rowan bark, a concoction of that would soon sort it out I'm sure."

Lavender gave a sigh, "Oh well, there's no point in wishing for what you can't have. Now, what was it you were asking? Oh yes, about Africa, and you're quite right that was when Horatio found Neville. Poor old chap; imagine being the last of your kind left in the world. It must be a very lonely existence, don't you think?"

Neville was a dodo, the last dodo in the world, and Horatio had come across him hiding in the forest, too afraid to venture out in case he too was killed by the humans, just like the rest of his race. Thanks to Horatio, the dodo now lived safely and peacefully on the island in the middle of the lake at the Valley of Jewels.

There was no response from her daughter, so Lavender repeated her question, "Don't you agree Petunia?"

"Um … what? Oh sorry Mama, I was thinking about something else. What were you saying?"

"Oh never mind," Lavender sighed and shook her head at her daughter's absentmindedness.

"Just take the stick to your father, while I go and attend to the nippy, the poor thing must be fed up with waiting. And tell Horatio to rest his leg as much as possible," she called back over her shoulder as she hurried off.

Petunia made her way to where her father was patiently waiting, and delivered both the stick and her mother's message. Horatio invited her to go with him to the nursery to inspect the young plants he was growing, normally there was nothing Petunia enjoyed more than strolling round the garden listening to her father's stories about how he had discovered this plant or that shrub; but today, much to his surprise, she declined his offer. Something Lavender had said earlier had given Petunia an idea, an exciting idea, and she was anxious to begin to put it into action.

"No thank you Papa. I won't come with you today, if you don't mind. I thought I might go and visit Magenta, I haven't seen her for such a long time."

"Of course my dear, I quite understand," Horatio smiled fondly down at his daughter. "Much more fun to spend

99

some time with someone your own age rather than an old fuddy-duddy like me; off you go then, enjoy yourself. Give my regards to Rufus and Ariadne, if you should see them."

"Oh Papa, you are silly," said Petunia, giving him a kiss and feeling a little guilty at not telling the whole truth. "You're not a fuddy-duddy at all. But before I go, I would just like to ask you a question. You don't have any rowan trees in the garden, do you?"

Horatio gave a sigh. "No I'm afraid not and it's something I really regret. You see, because the trees were used to mark the portals between the two worlds, they were always so handy and I never saw the necessity to grow any here. Of course, once that was all gone, the portals closed and the trees destroyed, I realised my mistake, but it was too late. Why this sudden interest, may I ask?"

"Oh, it's just that Mama was saying how much she wished she could make a concoction of rowan bark to bathe your poor leg."

"Oh yes, marvellous stuff for ulcers, and rowan tea is just wonderful if you're suffering from indigestion or an upset tummy, nothing quite like it."

As if to demonstrate, Horatio gave a small burp. "Oh pardon me," he said, putting his paw over his mouth. "There, you are you see, I shouldn't have mentioned it, just the thought gets me going."

"Are there no trees left in the Wide World at all?" asked Petunia.

"I believe there maybe, up in the mountains. As you know from your history lessons, not all the humans wanted the dragons to go; and although many human lifetimes have passed since the banishment, and people have probably forgotten all about dragons  now, I should think the trees will have survived."

Petunia felt a surge of excitement; could she do it, could she? If she could find some rowan tree berries and bring them back to the Inner World, just imagine. She wouldn't be silly, absentminded Petunia then, would she? She took a deep breath, to calm herself down, there was a lot more planning to do yet.

Petunia said goodbye to Horatio and flew off to the Valley of Jewels in search of Magenta. The red dragon wasn't hard to find, she and her father, Rufus, were in the courtyard of their palace counting jewels. The piles of gemstones twinkled and sparkled so much in the sunshine that Petunia was temporarily blinded by their brilliance, and nearly landed on top of the nippy that was busy polishing them.

"Tunie! What a lovely surprise," Magenta greeted her, screwing up her eyes against the glare of the stones. "Have you come to tea? I do hope so."

"Hello Magenta. Hello Sir, my father sends his regards."

Petunia nodded at Rufus, who smiled back at her in a vague fashion, as he noted down a figure on a piece of paper bark.

"Tea would be nice, but I really just came for a chat, it's such a long time since I've seen you." Petunia squinted at her friend. "Do you think we could go outside for a walk? It's so bright in here; I don't know how you stand it."

"Is that alright, Papa?" Magenta asked her father.

"Yes, yes, you two run along, I'm almost finished here anyway."

The two young dragons went through the palace's main gate and began to walk down towards the lake. The Valley of Jewels was as beautiful and as perfect as ever, brightly coloured birds sang in the trees and there were flowers of every possible colour. Not one leaf or blade of grass was out of place, everything gleamed. Petunia knew that it took a small army of nippies, constantly polishing and dusting to keep everything looking the way it was. Her thoughts turned to her parent's cosy cave, which had bunches of her mother's herbs hanging up to dry, and her father's flowerpots stacked by the door. Perfection was all very well, but it wasn't very homely.

They reached the edge of the water and stopped to watch a pair of purple swans glide majestically past, the gold crowns on their heads glinting in the sunlight.

Petunia nodded towards the island in the centre of the lake, and asked, "Do you see much of Neville?"

"I don't go often," Magenta replied. "He is such a strange creature, won't live anywhere else, despite Papa offering. Neville claims the island is the only place he feels safe."

"I found my father's journal about their trip to Africa, when they found him. It sounded such an exciting journey. Do you ever wonder what it must be like in the Wide World? Do you ever wish you could go there?"

Petunia regarded her friend closely and was disappointed to hear her reply.

"Never give it a moment's thought. Why would I want to go anywhere?" Magenta asked in astonishment. "I already live in the most beautiful place, and anyway we have the jewels to look after, and Papa likes to have them counted every day. 'Everything in its place, and a place for everything', is what he always says."

"Yes, but if it hadn't been for my father travelling and collecting all these wonderful trees and flowers, and the birds and the insects, of course, the Valley of Jewels wouldn't even be here."

"But it is, so I don't need to go anywhere, do I?"

"Oh."

Magenta looked at Petunia with puzzlement.

"Whatever are you on about Tunie? It's not even as if we could go if we wanted to. You know it's not allowed, and there isn't a portal left open anyway."

"But Ffain went, all those years ago to help the unicorns. He found a portal."

"Yes, apparently there was one behind the waterfall, but the humans closed it, filled it right in; and look at the trouble Ffain got into."

"I thought he was very brave."

"Brave, ha! Stupid more like, and he broke an oath."

Petunia, who thought that Ffain was not only brave but very handsome too, decided she had better change the subject.

"But wouldn't you like to go Madge? Just to have a peek. I wonder what a human really looks like. There must be a portal still open somewhere."

"Oh Tunie, you know what they look like, you've been told enough times. You really are being very silly. Peeking through a portal, how ridiculous! And anyway, there are none left, Papa told me, so there. Come on, let's go back and see if tea's ready, I'm starving."

Petunia was so disappointed with her lack of progress she hardly ate any tea at all, despite Magenta's mother, Ariadne, offering her plate after plate of the most delicious looking cakes and sweetmeats. She half listened to the red dragon family chatting to each other whilst the problem of how to find a portal went round and round in her head.

"You're very quiet Petunia dear, are you feeling unwell?" Ariadne asked with concern.

"I'm fine, thank you," Petunia replied.

"Loonie Tunie, dreaming about the Wide World, I expect," Magenta sang out.

"Magenta! Don't be unkind and stop talking nonsense," Ariadne turned on her daughter crossly.

"But it's true," Magenta objected. "Petunia said that she wanted to go to the Wide World."

Petunia glared at her friend from across the table. How could she be so mean, telling her secrets to everyone?

"I'm sure Petunia said no such thing," said Rufus kindly. "Did you my dear?"

"I did say that I wondered what the Wide World was like," Petunia admitted. And then she added bravely, "I think it's a shame that dragons aren't allowed to visit it anymore. I would like to see it."

"Well, well, you certainly are your parent's daughter. I suppose it's only natural that with Lavender and Horatio for a mother and father, you would inherit their love of travel. But I'm afraid you will have to be content with exploring the Inner World and, you know, there's a lot more to it than just the Kingdom of the High Mountain."

"That's a good idea," Ariadne nodded in agreement with her husband. "You could go exploring here; meet some new dragons, perhaps. I think the Wide World is best forgotten, after all just look at the narrow escape the poor unicorns had."

Petunia smiled in agreement but her mind was racing, the unicorns of course, she should have gone there first. She had got to know the unicorns well during the time she had spent helping her mother at the sanctuary, and there was one unicorn in particular with whom she had struck up a friendship, Mistral.

She would go and see Mistral.

As soon as she was able, Petunia said her farewells to the red dragons and flew out of the Valley of Jewels in search of the unicorn herd. She found them grazing in the area where a stream joined the river. She spotted Mistral standing with another young unicorn; Petunia flew down and landed near them.

"Hello Petunia. What a lovely surprise," her friend greeted her. "You know Sirocco, don't you?"

"Yes, of course. How are you, and your parents? All well, I hope."

"Fine, thank you," Sirocco answered politely. "Everyone's fine."

"And you Mistral? How are your family?"

"Very well, thank you Petunia."

Silence fell, the two unicorns regarded Petunia curiously, the dragon shifted about uncomfortably until Mistral took pity on her.

"Was there something you wanted? Surely you didn't fly all this way just to ask how we were."

"Um, no, I was wondering … er, I wanted to ask."

Petunia looked at Sirocco who was standing to one side with a bemused expression on his face. The dragon bent her head closer to Mistral.

"Is it possible to speak to you on your own?" she asked.

Mistral turned towards Sirocco who grinned good naturedly and announced, "I'll be off then, see you later."

With that the young unicorn turned and cantered away. Mistral watched him go.

"Ooh, he's so handsome, don't you think?"

She glanced up at Petunia and seeing the expression on her face, added, "Oh dear, this is serious, isn't it? Come on, let's go somewhere we won't be disturbed."

The two friends began to walk alongside the stream, back towards the hills. As they made their way Petunia explained to Mistral how she wanted to go into the Wide World to get some rowan bark and berries to help her father but was unable to because she didn't know where to find a portal.

Mistral felt sorry for her friend, she had noticed how often Petunia was scolded by Lavender for her day dreaming and absentmindedness. She had heard Magenta teasing her for the same reason, all of which had made the purple dragon less and less self-confident.

This became evident as Petunia exclaimed, "Oh, I don't know Mistral, maybe I am being silly as usual! Perhaps I should give up the whole idea. I expect everyone is right and I am just too stupid to do anything  useful, and besides it's not allowed."

"Now you are being silly," her friend scolded her gently. "You have a fine brain and a kind heart. Where would the harm be if you found a portal and went to the end of it to collect some bark and a few berries? Why, I don't suppose anyone would even realise you were gone. You'd probably be there and back again before anybody knew it."

They had reached a small clearing by some rocks; Petunia stopped walking and turned to Mistral in frustration.

"But that's the problem, you see. I don't know where there is a portal. Oh Mistral," Petunia slumped to the ground with disappointment. "Everybody's right, I am useless, aren't I? I can't even help my own father."

"Now, now, don't give up. I'm sure we can find a way to get you to the Wide World, if we just put our heads together."

"Three heads are better than two," said a voice.

The dragon and the unicorn jumped with surprise.

"Who's there?" asked Petunia nervously.

"Who are you, and where are you?" Mistral demanded crossly. "And how dare you eavesdrop on a private conversation."

"Begging your pardon, I'm sure," came the reply. "But you are standing right outside my house, so I'm afraid I couldn't help but overhear."

"Your house?"

Mistral looked around and saw a bright blue mouse standing near her on a ledge of rock.

"Yep, that's right," the mouse jerked a thumb back over one shoulder. "This is where I live."

Petunia and Mistral saw that there was an entrance to a small cave at the back of the ledge, but both of them were too amazed by the mouse's appearance to take much notice. Neither of them had ever seen another rainbow mouse like it. He was standing up on his hind legs on which he was wearing a pair of large brown boots. There was a belt fastened around his middle from which protruded what appeared to be several various types of weapons, and on his head he was wearing a rather oddly shaped hat. The mouse removed the hat with a flourish and made a bow as he announced.

"Montgomery Action Mouse at your service."

"What!" spluttered Mistral, trying not to laugh. "A what mouse?"

"Action Mouse," the mouse answered, replacing his hat with dignity. "But you may call me Monty."

"Um, what exactly does that mean Monty?" Petunia asked kindly. "What do you do?"

"Oh," Monty replied, in an offhand way. "Fight wars, rescue people, jump off tall buildings, cross crocodile infested rivers, wrestle with lions, swim in shark infested seas."

The little mouse counted each item off on his paws as he recited the list. At the mention of lions Mistral could contain herself no longer and burst into laughter. Petunia, not wanting to hurt Monty's feelings, fought to keep her face straight.

"I'm afraid I don't know what a crocodile or a shark is, but where do you do all this?"

"In the Wide World, of course," said Monty with a swagger. "Very well-known there I am, famous even. Oh yes, everyone in the Wide World knows Montgomery Action Mouse. You got any problems you want solving, I'm your mouse."

"So you go backwards and forwards to the Wide World all the time, do you?" Petunia asked.

"Of course," said Monty. "I spend half my life there."

"I'm surprised you bother to come back here at all," remarked Mistral. "It must be so boring after all that excitement."

"Well…yes," said Monty doubtfully. "But - but sometimes it's nice to have some peace and quiet, isn't it?"

He looked up at Mistral triumphantly.

"Oh yes, I'm sure you need the rest," she agreed smiling at him.

Petunia had other things on her mind. "Where do you go through, Monty? Is there a portal near here?"

"Of course," Monty boasted. "Right here, at the back of my cave."

"Where?" Petunia asked excitedly, trying to see into the cave. "Can I see it? Will I fit through?"

"Goodness me, no," the mouse gave a small laugh. "You'd get stuck, you would. It's only a small tunnel, comes out under a little boy's bed it does."

"A little boy's bed," repeated Mistral. "Yes, I see, there must be a lot of wars and people that need rescuing in a little boy's bedroom."

Monty looked down at his boots and then, deciding to ignore Mistral, he asked Petunia, "So you want to find a portal, do you?"

"Yes," said the dragon. "But one I can fit through, obviously. Do you know if there are any left?"

"I think I might know just the place, but it is quite a long way from here."

Petunia could not believe her luck, at last a chance to prove to everyone that she was neither silly nor stupid. She thought of Magenta and how surprised she would be when she heard that Petunia had been to the Wide World. She imagined the look on her parent's faces when she presented them with the rowan bark. And she thought of Ffain, she had only seen the young green dragon a few times since his return from the Wide World all those years ago, and then it had only been for brief periods whenever his parents had visited the sanctuary. Although she didn't really understand why, above all else Petunia wanted to be able to tell Ffain that she had been to the Wide World too.

"Where?" she demanded of the mouse. "Just tell me where and I'll go there."

"On the shore of the Silver Sea," Monty replied. "There is a large cave there and I believe there is a portal within it."

"The Silver Sea," repeated Petunia.

"Have you ever been there?" asked Monty.

Petunia shook her head

"Honestly, you dragons, I'll never understand you. You never go anywhere. Where's your sense of adventure?"

"Well, we can't all be fighting wars and rescuing people." Mistral spoke up in defence of her friend.

"How do I get there?" Petunia asked impatiently. "Which way is the Silver Sea?"

Monty shook his head in amazement at the dragon's ignorance. "Why you follow the river of course, the river flows to the Silver Sea."

Petunia turned to Mistral. "I've got to go; I've just got to go."

"But not on your own," her friend replied. "I'm coming with you."

Petunia looked at the unicorn in surprise.

"Coming with me?"

"Well I'd like to," Mistral offered. "But only if you

want me to of course."

Petunia felt a huge rush of relief.

"Oh yes, Mistral. Thank you, of course I want you to come."

The two friends smiled at each other.

"Ahem," Monty gave a small cough to remind them of his presence. "From one adventurer to another I would like to wish you good luck, and if you'd allow me …"

The mouse turned and scampered back into his cave. Petunia and Mistral just had enough time to exchange a mystified glance before he reappeared dragging a small bag by a long strap.

"I heard you mention collecting something, in which case you might find this useful."

"Oh Monty, how clever of you, I hadn't thought …" Petunia began to look downcast again.

"Now, now," Mistral admonished her. "We would have thought of something, but this is just the ticket. It looks as though it will fit, if you wouldn't mind helping."

Petunia lifted the strap over the unicorn's head and the bag slid down Mistral's neck until it came to rest snugly against her chest.

"A perfect fit Monty, thank you."

"Glad to be of service, if ever you need any help you know where to find me," Monty gave another bow, clicking his heels together and flourishing his hat at the same time. "Farewell and good luck."

With that the mouse turned and disappeared back into his cave.

"Thank you, thank you very much," Petunia called after him.

"What a strange little chap," Mistral remarked, echoing Petunia's own thoughts. "Well, I suppose we had better get going; after all there is nothing to stop us now."

Petunia felt a shiver run down her spine at the unicorn's words, her stomach suddenly felt as though it were full of butterflies. Could she do it? Could she really go to the Wide World? She looked at Mistral waiting patiently beside her with a questioning look on her face. What a good and loyal friend she was, and she was right, there was nothing to stop them now. Petunia took a deep breath and tried to put all her doubts and fears out of her mind.

"Yes, let's go."

The two friends retraced their steps to where the stream and the river met, the rest of the unicorn herd barely noticed them as they turned downstream and began to follow the river. Only Sirocco lifted his head and watched them pass, wondering where they were going.

As soon as they were out of sight Mistral broke into a trot and then a canter, Petunia took to the skies flying low over the unicorn as she followed the course of the river. The familiar hills and mountains soon began to disappear out of sight behind them as the river widened and slowed on its journey to the sea.

As they neared the river mouth the land on either side began to rise again. Looking ahead Petunia could see the rays of the evening sun sparkling on water and the ground beneath Mistral's hooves began to change from earth to sand. The river bank grew wider and wider until finally, it became a beach and all they could see in front of them stretching across the horizon was water. Mistral stopped and Petunia landed next to her on the sand.

"It's huge," remarked the dragon. "I never expected it to be so big. I wonder where it ends?"

"Enormous," Mistral agreed. She lifted one hoof

daintily from the wet sand. "And wet, yuk, I hate water. I hope the cave is on this side of the river, because I can't swim and it looks too deep to wade through."

"Goodness, I hadn't thought of that. How stupid of me, why on earth didn't I ask Monty? What will we do if you can't get across?" Petunia began to twist her paws together with anxiety.

"Now, now, don't go getting all worked up," said Mistral calmly. "We haven't even begun to look for the cave yet. Those cliffs over there look like a good place to start, come on."

They were in luck the cave was easy to find, the entrance lit up for them by the rays of the setting sun. Petunia, who had been worrying about arriving in the Wide World in the daylight, felt reassured. Maybe, she thought as they picked their way over the rocks to the tunnel at the back of the cave, everything is going to be alright after all.

PART 2. KIDNAPPED!

VII

The two friends emerged from the other end of the tunnel to find themselves on a steep hillside overlooking a large lake with an island in the middle. If it hadn't been such a cold and forbidding place it would have looked very similar to the lake in the Valley of Jewels, Petunia thought. But this was the Wide World; she felt a shiver of excitement run through her. The Wide World, at last she was really here.

Much to their relief there was no sign of any humans, they couldn't see any buildings or lights, in fact the whole area appeared to be uninhabited. The darkness was complete, broken only by the light of the full moon and the stars which floated high in the night sky looking down on their reflections in the waters of the lake. The dragon and the unicorn stood side by side looking around, taking note of their surroundings.

"Thank goodness for the moonlight," Mistral murmured, unwilling to break the silence.

But she needn't have worried because the words were barely out of her mouth before the peace of the night was shattered by Petunia who gave a squeal of delight as she ran off to one side.

"I don't believe it, I just don't believe it! Look Mistral, look, it's a rowan tree! Here, right here, the portal is marked by a rowan tree, just as they used to be in the old days."

By the time Mistral reached her side Petunia was already picking berries from the tree.

"I knew it, I knew it," the dragon said excitedly, as she began to put the berries in the bag around Mistral's neck. "Just wait till Mama sees these; she is going to be so pleased." A thought struck her. "You know Mistral," she said, as she began to peel some bark away from the tree before placing it in the bag with the berries. "I was just thinking, wouldn't it be wonderful to find some seedlings to take home for Papa's nursery. I'm sure we won't have to look too far to find some. This tree is so well established, there must be some young ones nearby."

Mistral stood still as Petunia fastened the bag. "Why don't we split up?" she suggested. "You go up and I'll go down towards the lake. We can both make a loop and meet back here."

With no more than a brief, "See you later," Petunia was off uphill determined to find some seedlings to take back to her beloved Papa. Mistral smiled at her friend's enthusiasm as she picked her way downhill. Dear Petunia, she wanted to please everyone so much. It was a shame she had so little confidence in her own abilities, but if taking rowan trees back to the Inner World was what she needed to boost her self-esteem then Mistral was determined to make their expedition a success.

The undergrowth became thicker as the unicorn neared the shore of the lake; Mistral began to walk more slowly, studying each small tree she passed in case one proved to be a rowan. So intent was she on her task she was unaware of the movement in the bushes around her and the fact that she was no longer alone until she was blinded by a bright light shining straight into her eyes. Mistral tried to turn away but something grasped the strap of the bag around her neck, stopping her in her tracks. Her instinct was to rear up but just as she tried to lift her front legs a rope was quickly wound round them, binding them together and forcing the unicorn to stand still in fear of losing her balance and falling over completely in the darkness.

She tried to cry out to Petunia but her cry was stifled as more rope was fastened around her nose and a further loop pulled up over her ears. It all happened in less than a minute but she found herself completely trapped.

At last the burning light was turned away from her eyes and redirected elsewhere. Mistral blinked trying to adjust her sight to the semi darkness. She was aware of a figure nearby, but it wasn't until she heard voices that her worse fears were confirmed. She had been captured by humans.

Mistral had only been a foal when the unicorns had fled into the Inner World, hundreds of human years had passed but she could remember enough of that terrifying time to know that not all humans could be trusted; there were good people and there were bad people. Listening to the conversation between the two humans who had captured her, she was in no doubt which sort they were.

"Blimey Billy boy, our luck's in tonight. Oo'd 'ave fort a bloomin' unicorn would come walking down the mountain."

"Told you I 'eard somefin, didn't I?" Billy panted. He was still breathing heavily from the effort of capturing Mistral.  "Must admit I just fort it was a stray pony that would fetch us a few quid at the market. Phew! I never expected this," he sunk to the ground, shaking his head in disbelief. "Just look at that 'orn."

The torch beam flashed over Mistral's face again, making her pull backwards against the rope clasped in Billy's hand. He jerked it roughly causing the unicorn to stumble forwards.

"That's real silver, that is," his friend pointed out. "Worth a fortune, much more than these stupid, old pheasants we've poached." He kicked out at something at his feet and Mistral realised there was a small pile of dead birds lying on the ground.

"Cor, wait till we get this 'ome. People always go on about strange things 'appening in these hills, but I never believed it until now. We're going to be rich Billy boy. Rich!"

"Now 'ang on a minute Dave, 'old yer 'orses, or should I say unicorns, ha, ha. Seriously we've got to fink this through; we can't just go turning up wiv a unicorn. People will be suspicious. To start wiv they'll want to know what we was doing wandering around the mountains in the dark."

"We could kill it now," Dave suggested. "'It it over the 'ead wiv a rock, cut off it's 'orn and we're 'ome and dry."

Mistral felt a cold shiver of fear run down her spine as she heard him speak so callously.

"No, Dave, no, that's exactly what I mean, yer not finking this through. Don'tcha fink that maybe this animal might be worth more to us alive? Just fink what people would pay to see a real, live unicorn."

"Oh yeah, I 'adn't thought of that, good idea. 'Ere, what's that fing round its neck? There's somefin' on that strap you grabbed hold of, looks like a camera bag to me."

"Don't be stupid," Billy replied, getting to his feet. "Unicorn with a camera, whatever are you on about?" He shone his torch on the bag. "Well blow me, I think yer right. What's goin' on?"

He reached out for the bag and Mistral jerked her head away. Billy pulled hard on the rope halter forcing the unicorn's nose back down towards him.

"You keep still and let me 'ave a look," he growled at her threateningly.

He fumbled with the catch on the bag, managed to get it open and shone the torch inside.

"What is it Billy? What's in there?"

"Just a load of old berries and bits of bark, rowan berries, I 'fink. Now, what's that all about?"

Dave gave a gasp. "Rowan? That's the witches' tree that is. I wouldn't touch that if I were you, it might be a spell or somethin'. 'Ere, maybe it's a witches' unicorn, yer don't 'fink there's one wiv it, do yer? "

He began to look around nervously.

"Don't be so stupid," said Billy. Even so he fastened the bag up carefully and took a step away from Mistral.

"Maybe we should just let it go, Billy," Dave fretted. "Maybe it's cursed."

Mistral felt her

heart leap at his words, but her hopes were soon dashed.

"Stop goin' on and giv'us a minute to work out a plan. I'm not going to give up that easily."

Billy pushed his greasy cap backwards and scratched his head; silence fell. Mistral tried to move slowly away, but Billy had a tight hold on the end of the rope halter and the hobble around her forelegs only allowed her to hop slightly backwards.

"You 'ang on, my beauty," Billy spoke to her. "I've got big plans for you."

"Shame there's not a nuvver one, eh Billy? We could breed 'em, set up our own unicorn farm," Dave chuckled.

"Better keep yer eyes peeled then Dave. Yer never know yer luck."

Mistral thought about Petunia, surely she must be missing her by now. The unicorn didn't know whether to wish her friend would appear, or to hope she stayed away. Mistral had never felt so afraid in all her life. Whatever was going to happen to her?

"Got it," Billy announced, slapping his thigh with one hand. "I saw a boat back there a ways, quite a big 'un. We'll get 'er in there and row 'er over to the island. She won't be able to get off there and no one will be able to find 'er neiver. In the morning I'll come back wiv the lorry, we'll load 'er up and, Bob's yer uncle, job done!"

"Good plan Billy boy, good plan."

"Right, let's get going. You go back along the lake, find the boat and bring it 'ere. Then we'll work out 'ow to persuade our friend 'ere to get in. I've got an idea 'bout that an' all."

Dave took his torch from his pocket and switched it on before disappearing into the bushes. Billy picked up a stout stick that was lying beside the bodies of the pheasants and stepped closer to Mistral. He laid his hand on her neck; the unicorn shuddered under his touch.

"Now, now my beauty," Billy murmured. "You come along wiv me; we're going to do a little experiment, you an' me."

He took a step forwards and pulled on the rope halter fastened around Mistral's head, the unicorn resisted until Billy lifted the stick and brought it down sharply behind her knees. The pain shot up the unicorn's legs and into her shoulders, her knees buckled and she fell forward onto the ground.

"We can do this the 'ard way, or the easy way. It's up to you," Billy remarked.

Mistral struggled to push herself back up off the ground; she managed it at last and stood panting with effort.

"Now then," said Billy. "Let's try again, shall we? Come along."

He pulled on the halter again, this time Mistral hopped forward behind him.

"That's my girl, well done, just a little further."

In this fashion Billy led Mistral towards the lake stopping at the edge. Mistral stood trembling miserably beside him, her flanks covered in sweat partly from fear and partly from the effort it had taken to get there.

The water looked cold, dark and uninviting.

"Now, let's see what yer fink of this."

Without any warning Billy swept the cap from his head, through the water and in one movement threw the cap of water over Mistral. The unicorn panicked as the icy water hit her, snorting with terror she tried to rear up which caused her to fall heavily onto the stony ground where she lay gasping with pain and shock, her poor bruised body aching from limb to limb.

"Well, well, well," remarked Billy. "I reckon all those old wives tales me great granny used to tell me about unicorns bein' afraid of water are true."

There was a splashing noise from the lake and a boat, being rowed by Dave, came into view. He gave a final push through the water with the oars and the boat glided gently up onto the shore beside them.

Billy turned back to Mistral as Dave clambered out of the boat.

"Well, my darlin', what's it to be? You either get into the boat like a good girl, or we tie you on and drag you across. Fancy a swim, do you?"

"Blimey Billy, yer talking to 'er as if she can understand yer," Dave remarked.

"Oh, don't you worry Dave, me old mate, she understands alright. She understands everything I've said."

Billy looked straight into Mistral's eye. "Well?"

The unicorn knew it was hopeless trying to get away, her only hope lay in Petunia, but where was she? Mistral nodded once.

"That's more like it, now yer being sensible. Right

Dave, come and give us a hand, let's get this beauty into the boat."

Billy knelt down and began to loosen the hobble on Mistral's legs. From her hiding place in the bushes Petunia watched in growing horror as the two men manhandled the exhausted unicorn into the boat and began to row across the lake.

She had been so happy waiting for Mistral to join her back at the tunnel entrance, impatient to show the unicorn the two fine young rowan tree seedlings she had found to take back for Horatio. She had been imagining the looks on her parents' faces when she presented them with their gifts. Lost in her daydreams it was only when the movement of the moon across the night sky caused its light to shine directly in her face that she realised just how late it was getting, and how long Mistral had been missing.

Petunia placed the seedlings carefully behind some rocks and began to make her way down towards the lake. She hadn't gone far before she heard a voice and water splashing, followed by the thump of something falling heavily onto the stones of the lakeside. Peering cautiously round some bushes Petunia was shocked to see Mistral, her forelegs tied together, struggling to get up onto her feet whilst a man stood beside her holding onto a rope halter that was fastened around the unicorn's head. Petunia could hardly believe her eyes, this just couldn't be happening, there must be some mistake. She watched in growing horror as another man appeared out of the darkness rowing a boat across the lake and then the pair of them proceeded to force Mistral into it.

Do something, I've got to do something, she thought, but at the same time she felt terribly afraid. Breathe fire? No, the men were far too close to Mistral and besides she wasn't sure she could actually hurt another living thing, all her life she had been taught to heal and nurture, to do deliberate harm to someone just wasn't in her nature.

Petunia's confusion and desperation grew as she saw the boat begin to draw away from the shore, back across the lake. One man was rowing, the other standing in the bows shining a light ahead over the water. One thing she knew without any doubt, whatever happened she had to keep them in sight. She stepped out cautiously onto the lakeside, afraid there may be other humans around; the boat had almost disappeared into the darkness. Petunia spread her wings and flew up into the night sky, low enough to be able to see the boat, but hopefully high enough not to be spotted.

She needn't have worried Billy and Dave were far too busy concentrating on getting across to the island to look up. Mistral stood shaking with fear in the centre of the boat, too terrified to move as she felt the movement beneath her and heard the water lapping against the sides of the boat. At last the boat grounded on the shore of the island. Billy quickly jumped out, splashing through the shallow water. He held onto the bow of the boat to steady it and called out to Dave.

"Okay, take off the rope."

Dave removed the hobble from Mistral's forelegs, for an instant she hesitated, unmoving.

"Go on my beauty, jump for it," Dave encouraged her.

The tired unicorn gathered the last of her strength and sprung over the side of the boat onto the shore, almost collapsing with relief as she felt solid ground beneath her hooves again. Billy caught hold of the halter as she landed.

"There we go, that's the way to do it, dry as a bone. Yer really don't like the water do yer? I don't fink I'll 'ave to worry too much about yer going anywheres. Even so we'll just make sure and besides, we don't want no one spotting yer from the shore, do we? 'Ang on 'ere Dave, I'll be back in a minute."

With that Billy turned and began to lead Mistral away from the shoreline. The island was thickly wooded, the trees growing so closely together that several times Billy was forced to lead the unicorn this way and that weaving between their trunks. Mistral stumbled along behind him, tripping over roots and ducking under low branches, too worn out to do anything but follow. At last Billy was satisfied that they were far enough away from the shore, he stopped and tied Mistral up firmly to the trunk of a tree. Then he patted her on the neck, saying.

127

"Good night my beauty, have a good rest and I'll see yer in the morning bright and early." He gave a low chuckle. "Make sure yer get yer beauty sleep now, big day tomorra, big day for all of us."

With that he turned and began to retrace his steps through the trees. Mistral stood with her head hanging down, the cuts and bruises where she had fallen and Billy had hit her, aching and sore, she felt utterly exhausted and very afraid. Whatever was going to happen to her?

From her vantage point in the sky Petunia saw the unicorn jump from the boat and watched one of the men lead her away, out of sight, into the woods. The other man leaned against the boat, smoking a cigarette while he waited. Petunia wondered what would happen next, why had they brought Mistral here?

During the time of the war between the lions and the unicorns, as she went about her work in the healing sanctuary, Petunia had once overheard some of the unicorns talking amongst themselves in lowered voices about their comrades who had been captured by the lion's army and suffered terribly in the hands of the men. She knew that the gold and silver unicorn horns were highly prized by humans. Had Mistral been brought here to suffer a similar fate? A terrible cold fear clutched at the dragon's heart when she thought of her friend being butchered in that fashion. She began to feel desperate, I will just have to set fire to everything, she thought, the whole island. It would be better for Mistral to die in that way than any other.

Then, to her relief, the second man reappeared from

the trees empty handed and re-joined his friend. The two of them climbed back into the boat and began to row away across the lake. Petunia let out the breath she had been holding, wherever Mistral was at least she was still in one piece. The dragon waited until the boat was completely out of sight and she could no longer hear the splashing of the oars in the water; then she began to fly low over the island. The trees grew so closely together it was impossible for her to see anything on the ground and there was nowhere for her to land.

She began to call out softly, "Mistral, Mistral, where are you? Can you hear me?" as she flew backwards and forwards above the trees.

Dazed with shock, cold and tired, Mistral had fallen into a doze. She dreamt she was back in the Inner World with the herd. She heard her mother calling her and tried to run to her, but something was stopping her. She tried harder and harder and almost fell as the rope around the tree snapped tight, jerking her awake. The memory of the dreadful ordeal she had been through came flooding back. If only this was a dream, she thought, a terrible nightmare from which I could wake up. But then she heard it again, someone was calling her name, it was Petunia. At last Petunia had come to help her.

"Petunia, I'm here, I'm here!" Can you see me?" Mistral stamped her hooves and swished her tail, moving around as much as the rope would allow her to, in the hope that the dragon would be able to spot her through the thick canopy of the trees.

Petunia was growing increasingly frustrated and was beginning to wonder if, indeed, she was too late to save her friend, when she thought she heard something. She hovered slowly trying to move her wings as little as possible as she listened. Then she heard it, Mistral calling out to her and, almost at the same time, she spotted a flash of white amongst the trees.

"Mistral, are you alright? I think I can see you, but I can't land, the trees are too close together. Can you hear me? Are you alright?"

The unicorn almost collapsed with relief at the sound of her friend's voice.

"Yes. Yes, I'm okay. Oh I'm so glad you found me, but whatever are we going to do Petunia? I'm tied up

and even if I wasn't I couldn't get across the water. The men will be back in the morning." She gave a sob of despair. "It's no good; you'll just have to go back without me."

The sound of her friends' desperation did something to Petunia, for the first time in her life she felt clear headed, determined and … angry, so angry. She had no doubts about what she had to do, she had got Mistral into this mess and she was going to get her out of it; and she knew who to ask for help.

"Mistral," she called down urgently to the unicorn. "Mistral listen to me, you mustn't give up hope. I'm going to get Ffain, he'll know what to do. Together we will get you out of here, you will go home, trust me. I'll be back as soon as I can."

Without waiting for a reply Petunia soared up into the sky, flying faster than she had ever done in her life. Mistral heard the determination in the dragon's voice and felt a glimmer of hope. At least something was happening, someone knew where she was; but Ffain, what on earth was he going to do? Mistral sighed, and tried to settle her aching body more comfortably, it was going to be a long wait.

PART 3. A BOY, A HUMAN BOY!

VIII

Petunia was aware of nothing except the wind rushing past her wings as she drove herself on through the night towards the tunnel entrance. At last she reached it and scrambled through back to the Inner World as fast as she could. She had barely cleared the mouth of the cave before she spread her wings and was airborne again. The same few words kept repeating over and over in her head as she pushed on through the night, flying low, following the river back to the mountains. 'Got to find Ffain, I've got to find Ffain.'

Petunia's wings were starting to tire but she wouldn't allow herself to even think about slowing down. Instead she concentrated on the rhythm of her flying, pushing her wings through the air, up and down, up and down. 'Got to find Ffain, I've got to find Ffain.'

She was almost at the waterfall when it happened, thinking about it afterwards she couldn't believe her luck and, how close she had come to missing him. A shadow passed between her and the moon, temporarily blocking the light she had been following reflected in the river. A cloud perhaps, but something made Petunia look up and she could hardly believe what she saw. The silhouette of a dragon passing across the face of the full moon, and she was sure she knew which dragon. Ffain, it had to be Ffain.

She tried to call out but couldn't find the breath she needed, the cool night air just seemed to dry up in her scorched throat as she quickly circled round to follow him, determined to keep him in sight and hoping desperately that he wouldn't be going too far. Despite being so tired, Petunia managed to keep Ffain in sight, but the gap between them was beginning to increase. The purple dragon was gasping for breath; the air seemed to grow heavier with every beat of her wings. Just as she thought she was going to have to give up, at last, to her relief, she saw Ffain begin to drop downwards preparing to land somewhere near the river.

Ffain was looking for Sirocco; the two of them had become the best of friends since Ffain had helped the unicorns in their flight from the Wide World. When he got time away from his duties in the High Kingdom the green dragon would often fly to wherever the herd happened to be and spend a few enjoyable hours in the company of the unicorn.

Tonight the herd were grazing by a bend in the river, where it was joined by a small stream. Ffain spotted Sirocco standing on his own, away from the others, staring downstream as if lost in thought. The unicorn hardly moved as the dragon landed neatly beside him and began to greet him.

"Hello Sirocco, how …"

"Ffain, I'm so glad you're here. There's something going on, I don't suppose you've seen Mistral anywhere, have you? Or Petunia for that matter?"

"Mistral? Petunia? Er, no, why should I?" Ffain asked, rather taken aback by the unicorn's question. "What do you mean, there's something going on?"

"Well, earlier today … goodness me!" Sirocco's explanation was cut short as Petunia tumbled from the sky and landed beside them, causing a cloud of dust to rise up. The purple dragon's sides were heaving as she looked wildly from Sirocco to Ffain and back again.

"Help!" she gasped, and then began coughing and spluttering as she breathed in some dust. "Mistral … tied up … island … you must come," she wheezed, her eyes watering and tears rolling down her face.

"Petunia, what on earth is the matter?" Ffain asked with some concern. "Just take a minute and get your breath, we can't understand what you are saying."

"Did you say Mistral's on an island?" asked Sirocco. "Have you been playing some silly game in the Valley of Jewels?"

Petunia felt a spurt of anger at Sirocco's words, how dare he assume she and Mistral had been playing games. She glared at the unicorn, but before she could open her mouth to speak, Ffain touched her gently on the shoulder.

"Let's move out of this dust, shall we? Somewhere a little quieter, where you can tell us all about it; we're beginning to attract attention."

Petunia looked round and realised that some of the other unicorns were looking across at them, wondering what all the fuss was about. She allowed Ffain to lead her along the side of the stream away from their curious stares, Sirocco following along behind. Once they were out of earshot, Ffain suggested that Petunia should have a drink and then tell them what was going on. Grateful for his concern the purple dragon took a long drink from the cool water of the stream and then, feeling a lot more composed, she proceeded to tell them all that had happened to her and Mistral that night.

Ffain and Sirocco were astonished by her story.

"You did what!" the green dragon blurted out as she described their passage through to the Wide World.

"Humans!" Sirocco said in horror when she mentioned Billy and Dave.

But they both remained silent when she finished her sorry tale and the seriousness of Mistral's predicament became clear. Petunia could tell they were both thinking hard and, for the first time since she had left Mistral, she began to feel slightly less afraid. She was glad Ffain had been with Sirocco, three heads had to be better than two, and she knew how resourceful the two of them could be. Sirocco was the first to speak.

"I could go in her place," he suggested. "Give myself to the humans instead of her."

Petunia's heart went out to him. He really cares for her, she thought.

"A noble offer, my friend; but who's to say we wouldn't end up losing both of you," said Ffain. "Just let me think, there must be another way."

"We must hurry," Sirocco said impatiently. "Petunia said they are coming back in the morning. I know time passes differently in the Wide World, but we'll be losing the cover of darkness soon."

Petunia glanced anxiously at each of their faces in turn. Ffain began to question her.

"She's on an island?"

"Yes."

"And there is definitely nowhere to land?"

"No, the trees are too dense."

"And she is tied up?"

"Yes."

"If we could burn through the rope, could she swim across?"

"No," this was from Sirocco. "Unicorns have a great fear of water and Mistral is worse than most of us in that respect."

"What about carrying her?" suggested Petunia.

An image rose up in Ffain's and Sirocco's minds of Black Mane dangling lifelessly from the green dragon's talons.

Ffain cleared his throat, "Ahem, it would be difficult to hold her securely without harming her, but it may be possible."

"What about getting one of the donzels, Sable perhaps, to row the boat?" Sirocco suggested.

"It is quite a big boat," Petunia said doubtfully.

"We haven't enough time to get them and besides at the moment I think the fewer of us that know about this the better," Ffain pointed out.

The three of them fell silent as they thought about the consequences of their parents learning what had happened. A voice, that only Petunia recognised, interrupted their thoughts.

"I know someone that could row a boat and untie a rope."

"Monty!" she exclaimed.

The mouse stepped out from the shadows, where he had been standing listening to their conversation, and gave Petunia a bow.

"I'm sorry to hear about your friend, it seems as though she needs rescuing. This sounds like a job for Monty Action Mouse!"

"Oh good grief," said Ffain, looking down at Monty in his boots and hat. "Whatever next?"

"Come on," urged Sirocco. "We've wasted enough time; we've got to get going."

"But you don't understand," said Petunia. "It's what Monty does, he's always rescuing people. Aren't you Monty?"

"But … he's a mouse!" spluttered Ffain.

"Ah, yes," said Monty in agreement. "But a mouse

with a plan." He held up one paw. "Please wait, just give me a few moments, that's all I ask, and then you'll see."

With that Monty turned on his heels and marched off into his cave. Ffain and Sirocco looked at each other in amazement.

"What was that all about?" Ffain asked.

"He can't possibly help, he's only a mouse," said Sirocco.

"Please," begged Petunia. "Please just give him a little time like he asked. After all we haven't got a better plan, have we?"

Sirocco and Ffain had to admit that this was true and they reluctantly agreed to give the mouse a short while to come up with something.

"Now this is the part of the story you've been waiting for, this is where I come in," Edward said, smiling at his son. He stretched out his legs which were feeling rather cramped from sitting for so long. "Do you want me to carry on, or shall I finish it another day?"

Toby and Sox had been so enthralled with the story, neither of them had so much as moved a muscle while they were listening, but now they chorused together.

"Please don't stop Dad; I want to know what happened."

"Please go on Mr.Edward, I must find out what happened to my Mum and Dad."

"Very well."

I was in bed reading, I knew I should have turned my light off hours ago but I had reached such an exciting point in my book I just had to carry on to find out what happened next. I had switched off my bedside light when I'd heard my parents coming up the stairs to go to bed, and I'd pretended to be asleep when my mother had put her head around the door to check all was well before closing it and turning off the landing light. I lay still for a few more minutes after hearing my parent's bedroom door shut, just to make sure they had really settled down for the night. I looked at the figures on my digital clock glowing in the dark, 10.43. I decided I would read until eleven o'clock, so I switched the

bedside light back on, pulled my book out from under the duvet, settled myself comfortably back on the pillows and started to try and find where I had got to.

I had just found my place on the page when a movement from the other side of the room caught my eye. I looked over at the window, but there was nothing there; it must have been a draught moving the curtains I thought, and turned back to the book. There it was again, something moving. It wasn't the curtains at all, it was on my desk, something was moving on my desk. It looked like a figure, a small figure, and it was … I screwed up my eyes and shook my head in disbelief; thinking it must be a trick of the light. Then I reopened my eyes, blinked several times and took another look. It was gone, just as I'd thought, a trick of the light.

I had almost settled back against my pillow when I saw it again, standing on the carpet between my bed and the desk. This time there was no mistake, it was a small figure and it was waving. No, not waving, beckoning, it was beckoning me to come closer. I crawled forward on my hands and knees until I reached the end of the bed, never taking my eyes off the creature that was now standing still as if it were waiting for me. It looked vaguely familiar in a strange sort of way. I examined it more closely, it was a mouse, I was sure of that, even if it was standing up on its' back legs … but what on earth?

"Action Man," I said to myself in disbelief. "It's wearing my Action Man boots and hat!"

Well, that was one mystery solved, I had been looking for my Action Man accessories for ages, in fact they'd been missing for months. I reached one hand slowly towards the mouse; it appeared to be watching quite calmly, with no sign of concern. Just as I thought it was within my grasp, the mouse skipped nimbly to one side avoiding my fingers, gave me a cheeky wink, beckoned once more and disappeared under the bed.

I didn't hesitate, a winking, beckoning mouse, what on earth was going on? I grabbed my torch from the top of the bookshelves and, switching it on, threw myself under the bed. Unfortunately the torchlight was weak because I had forgotten to change the batteries, but I could just make out that something was moving in the far corner. I pushed a couple of marbles and an empty Action Man box out of the way and wriggled forward on my stomach. It seemed very dark in the corner and I was glad I'd brought the torch, even if it wasn't giving out much light. How much further could it be? I reached out my hand to feel for the wall, but it felt more like rock, cold, damp rock.

I was just beginning to think that this was all too weird and that maybe I should crawl back out when I felt himself being pulled forward, faster and faster. I tried to resist but there was nothing I could do. Then, as suddenly as it had started, it stopped. I was no longer moving, but where was I? I sat up slowly and moved the weak beam of the torch around. It looked like a cave, I was sitting on dry earth, surrounded by rocks and in front of me I could just make out what must be the opening, I could even see a few stars twinkling in the sky.

I tried to make sense of what had happened. Could a mouse, I wondered, make a hole under my bed that was big enough for me to fall through into the garden? But even as I tried to convince myself I knew that this couldn't be the

case. A hole this size in my Dad's garden? No, someone would have seen it, but for the moment I could think of no other explanation. Then I thought I heard a voice, so I switched off the torch and crept quietly towards the opening of the cave to listen.

"This is ridiculous, Petunia," someone was saying. It was the deepest male voice I had ever heard. It was, I thought, the sort of voice you'd expect a giant to have.

"We have wasted quite enough time. Sirocco is right, we need to leave now, or it will be too late, the night will be over."

"Oh please Ffain," a lighter more feminine voice, that I assumed must be Petunia. "I'm sure Monty will be back soon, a few more …"

"And, here I am," a high pitched voice announced.

"At last, can we please get going now?" another male voice, but not so deep as the first. I thought I heard restless hooves striking the ground. Was it someone on horseback? Were they robbers? Don't be ridiculous, I told myself, robbers had getaway cars, not horses. I really could make no sense of it at all, but what I heard next, took my breath away. It was the deep voice again, Ffain.

"Well mouse, we waited as you asked. This had better be good, this plan of yours. I hope you haven't been wasting our time."

"No Sir, not at all, I can assure you."

The mouse could speak! I was astonished.

"For goodness sake, will you get on with it," the second male said impatiently. "Just tell us how you intend to row the boat across the lake and untie Mistral?"

"Why, I brought a boy, Sir. A boy can row a boat and

untie knots," Monty stated as if it were the most obvious thing in the world.

I heard a gasp of surprise from outside the cave, while at the same time I felt as though my stomach had tied itself into a hundred knots. What did he mean 'brought a boy'?

Ffain was asking the same thing. "A boy! You brought a human boy here?"

"Yes, he's just inside my cave. I don't know why he hasn't come out, maybe he's a bit shy. I'll go and get him, shall I?"

I looked quickly round for something to hide behind, but there was nothing. I turned to retreat back to where I had come from but before I could move a voice from somewhere near my feet said, "Hello again."

I looked down at the mouse I had seen in my bedroom - at least I thought it was the same mouse, even in the moonlight I could tell there was something different about it. I switched on the torch, shone it on the mouse and stared at him in amazement.

"You ... you've gone yellow, and you can talk," I was so surprised my voice came out in a squeak.

The mouse looked down at his fur. "Oh yellow is it this time? I hadn't noticed, I must admit I much prefer blue, but there we are no choice in the matter. I'm Monty by the way, Monty Action Mouse."

"Those belong to *my* Action *Man*," I pointed out, and then thought, good heavens I'm talking to a mouse!

"Er, well, you see ..."

Before Monty could explain any further Ffain's voice boomed out.

"Is the boy there? Is he coming to help?"

"What does he mean help?" I asked. "And who is he anyway?"

"It's a mission, a rescue mission, we have to save her," Monty gabbled. "You must come quickly, the others will explain."

He turned to go and then, stopping, asked. "You can row a boat, can't you?"

I must be asleep, I thought. Yes that's it, I've fallen asleep and this is all a dream. A talking mouse wants to know if I can row a boat. Fine, that's fine; I'll just go along with it and see what happens next.

"Yes, I can."

"Good, I thought that you would. Come along, come along."

Monty trotted off and I followed him out of the cave more slowly. I could feel rock beneath my bare feet and a cool breeze tugged at my pyjamas. It all seemed very real for a dream. I heard Petunia's voice saying.

"It is a boy, a real live boy!"

Her voice seemed to come from below me and I realised the rock formed a ledge and the owners of the voices I had heard were a little way below me. The torchlight was so weak now it was almost useless; I peered into the semi darkness and could just make out something large in the shadows, but I couldn't see any people.

"I think I had better go first."

It was the second male; once again I heard the sound of hooves as he came closer. The figure of a magnificent white horse emerged from the shadows and drew level with the ledge.

"My name is Sirocco."

I pointed the weak beam of the torch onto the horse's back, there was no one there.

"We need your help, are you one of Pendragon's men?"

I swung the torch round wildly, as the voice spoke again. I still couldn't find a person but something reflected the light back at me, glowing softly in the dim beam. Gold! A golden horn and below it a kind eye regarded me steadily.

"A unicorn!" I gasped.

"Yes," Sirocco agreed. "And you are obviously not a follower of Pendragon, but will you still help us? Please, I must know, one of my herd is in great danger."

I stared at Sirocco. It's not real, I thought, it's not real, this is just a dream. I cautiously reached out my arm and laid my hand gently on the unicorn's neck. It was warm and the soft skin quivered slightly under my touch. Sirocco turned his head and I felt the unicorn's breath against my face.

"You're real, you are a real unicorn."

My legs suddenly felt weak and I had to sit down, the ground was cold and solid through my pyjama trousers. There was a lump in my throat and I had to swallow hard before I could speak. I looked at Monty standing beside me, a bright yellow mouse, wearing Action Man's hat and boots, a plastic belt stuffed with toy guns and knives around his waist, Monty smiled at me.

"You're real too, I'm not dreaming, am I? What is this place? Where am I?"

"This is the Inner World," Sirocco said softly. "I am a

unicorn and this," he gave a sigh, "is a rainbow mouse. Tell me my friend, what is your name?"

"Edward," I replied in a daze. I drew up my knees, circled them with my arms and, closing my eyes, rested my head on them. It was all too much, I felt lonely and afraid, and I wished I was back in my bed, anywhere but here.

"Edward," Sirocco spoke to me urgently. "I understand this is a lot for you to take in, but we really do need your help. I would like to introduce you to my friends but first I want to reassure you that no one here will do you any harm. We want to be your  friends, we need your help. Do you understand?"

I felt a soft tapping on my foot, and looked down to see Monty patting me with his paw and smiling up at me in a reassuring way. I looked at Sirocco who was regarding me steadily, with a concerned look on his handsome face. They certainly didn't look as if they meant to hurt me and I realised that they really must need me to help with whatever it was. After all Monty had come especially to get me, hadn't he? The Inner World, Sirocco had said, I had read stories about other worlds never dreaming that one might actually exist. It would be an adventure, I thought, just like in my books; perhaps I should at least hear what it was they wanted me to do, after all I could always change my mind, but there was one thing I wanted to be sure of first.

"Can I go back to my world, when I want to?"

"Of course anytime, as long as there is a portal. We used to go backwards and forwards to the Wide World all the time in the old days."

"Some of us still do," Monty piped up.

"Hmph," Sirocco snorted. "Yes, well we can explain all about that to him later, when we have more time. Edward, are you ready to meet my friends now?"

"Yes," I said getting to my feet. I was starting to feel slightly better about things now I knew I could get back home whenever I wanted.

"Ffain, Petunia," Sirocco called out softly.

Something moved in the shadows, I was expecting more unicorns to step forwards, but the two shapes coming towards the ledge were much bigger than Sirocco, in fact they were huge, in fact they were …

"Dragons!" I exclaimed nervously, taking a few steps back nearer the safety of the cave.

"There's no need to be afraid," Sirocco reassured me. "This is Petunia and Ffain."

I looked at the dragons in awe, one was green and one was purple, I didn't need to ask which was which. The purple one had to be Petunia, there was something feminine about her and, although she was extremely large, the green dragon, Ffain, stood a head higher and half as wide again, he was the most awesome, terrifying creature I had ever seen. Petunia was the first to speak.

"I'm so pleased to meet you; I've never met a human before. I do hope we can be friends."

She had beautiful green eyes and she looked at me in such a kindly fashion I began to feel less afraid.

"N-Nice to meet you," I stammered, unsure of the right way to greet a dragon.

Ffain peered down at me, I noticed with a start, that his eyes were yellow and they glimmered coldly in the moonlight.

"Not much of you, is there? Are you sure you can help, boy?"

I drew himself upright and stood as tall as I could.

"My name is Edward and I'm above average height for my age," I said indignantly. "And besides, no one has explained exactly what you want me to do yet."

"And how old are you?" asked Ffain.

"Ten."

"Really, as old as that," said Ffain with a chuckle. "Well, I'm very pleased to meet you Edward. I just hope you are half as resourceful as the last human I had an adventure with."

My heart leapt at Ffain's words, if he knew other humans, perhaps they had visited this world too, but before I could ask any questions Ffain spoke again.

"I'm sorry to have to rush you but, as Sirocco has already mentioned, this is a matter of some urgency. I'm afraid you will have to put your trust in us, you have my word that we will do all we can to keep you from harm. One of the unicorns is trapped on an island; we need someone who can row a boat to rescue her. Can you do that?"

It was obvious to me that Ffain was someone used to being in charge; his commanding presence was not just down to his size. I knew instinctively that I could trust him and that the dragon had not given his word lightly; he would protect me and keep me safe.

"Yes," I said without hesitation. "Yes I can."

"Oh thank you Edward, thank you," said Petunia, and before I knew what was happening, she reached out, closed her fore paws round me and hugged me up against her scales so tightly I could hardly breathe.

"I knew it, I knew it," shouted Monty, skipping around with glee.

Sirocco and Ffain exchanged a look of relief, which quickly changed to worried frowns when they heard me start to speak.

"But I have to go back first."

"What!"

"Why?"

Ffain and Sirocco chorused.

I smiled up at their worried faces and, lifting up one foot, pointed out.

"I need to get some shoes, warmer clothes and

change the batteries in my torch. It will only take a few minutes."

Seeing the looks of dismay on their faces, I added. "I promise."

"I accept your promise," said Ffain solemnly. "But please be as quick as you can. We need the cover of darkness, we must leave soon or the night will be over. We will explain everything to you on the way. Go now."

I turned and headed back into the cave, Monty running ahead to show me the way. The journey back through the tunnel was every bit as nerve wracking as the journey out, but at least this time I knew where I was going to end up. As soon as I crawled out from under the bed I went over to my chest of drawers and started to get changed. A tee shirt, some jeans, a warm roll neck jumper, I sat on the bed to pull on my socks and trainers; I had just pulled on the second sock when I stopped. I looked round the room, at my books and toys, all the familiar things I saw every day. I listened, the house was quiet, I could just faintly hear my father snoring from across the landing. It made me smile, Mum was always complaining about that. It was all so normal. I looked at the clock beside my bed, 10.45. No, that couldn't be right, I was sure it had said 10.43 the last time I had looked, and that had been ages ago, before ... well, before everything. It must have stopped; but while I was watching the end digit changed 10.46., impossible.

Had it been a dream? Had it really happened? I held up my hand and looked at it, had I really touched a unicorn? Been hugged by a dragon?

Something moved on the floor, a mouse, an ordinary brown mouse … standing up on its back legs and wearing Action Man's hat and boots. Monty grinned up at me and beckoned urgently, of course it had happened, what was I thinking of? They needed me, they had asked for my help - two dragons, a mouse and a unicorn.

I grinned back at Monty as I laced up my trainers. One more thing to do, I unscrewed the base of the torch and quickly replaced the batteries with fresh ones from my desk drawer. I flashed the bright beam at Monty who gave me a thumbs up, then I took one last look around my bedroom before turning to the mouse.

"Right, let's go."

PART 4. TO THE RESCUE

IX

Petunia, Ffain and Sirocco were relieved to see Monty and I return from the cave; at last they could get going.

"We have to fly to another portal," Ffain explained. "One we can all fit through."

I was confused. "You mean the missing unicorn is in another world?"

"Yes your world, the Wide World; Mistral has been captured by humans."

I almost felt disappointed, I had been expecting an adventure in a strange and exotic land, but it seemed as though I was just going to go back where I'd come from. However, Ffain's next words certainly stopped me feeling sorry for myself.

"We have to travel fast, Sirocco will have enough to worry about just concentrating on where he is putting his hooves in the dark, and Petunia has already done the journey once, so I will carry you. Can you climb up onto my back?"

I was lost for words; ride on a dragon's back? Never in my wildest dreams had I ever imagined doing such a thing. Fortunately the height of the rock ledge made things a little easier, Ffain lowered his head and I was able to throw one leg across his neck. I settled myself just above the dragon's wings and checked to make sure the strap of the torch was fastened securely around my wrist.

"Are you ready?" asked Ffain.

"Wait, wait, you can't go without me!"

It was Monty squeaking at us and hopping up and down with indignation.

"You can't leave me behind; you wouldn't have Edward if it hadn't been for me."

"You must admit he has got a point," said Petunia. She turned to the mouse. "If you really want to come there is something you are going to have to do first."

"For goodness sake Petunia, this is ridiculous," said Ffain impatiently. "We've wasted enough time as it is."

"Trust me this is important and it won't take a minute; Edward could you shine your torch over there, towards the stream. Come with me Monty, please."

I did as Petunia asked and, as she made her way to

the stream, I heard her mutter under her breath.

"I know I saw some around here earlier."

She began to search through the plants growing at the waters' edge.

"Ah, here they are."

The purple dragon held her paw out under Monty's nose and showed him the strange spikey looking flowers she had picked.

"What on earth are those?" he asked.

"They are Green Spider Orchids, don't worry they're not as scratchy as they look, you shouldn't have any trouble swallowing them with a good drink of water. You're not that big, so I should think two will be enough."

"What? Swallow them! Have you gone mad?" shouted Monty, beginning to back away. "Why on earth would I want to swallow them?"

"So you can talk to us in the Wide World of course, there is nothing like Green Spider Orchids to help with communication. Don't you think that might be rather important?" Petunia asked sweetly.

"Oh."

Monty looked over to where we were waiting; he desperately wanted to join us on our adventure.

"Come on, be brave," urged Petunia. "It won't be that bad and the effect is only temporary."

Monty knew he had no choice; he took the flower heads from her and knelt down beside the stream. He had one last look at the oddly shaped flowers that did indeed look a lot like spiders, before placing them in his mouth, taking a long drink of water and swallowing hard. It wasn't as bad as he had been expecting, the flowers slipped down his throat quite easily and tasted faintly grassy.

"Alright?" asked Petunia.

Monty only had time to nod as Ffain called out.

"Come along, whatever are you doing?"

"Green Spider Orchid," Petunia explained as they hurried back towards us. "I thought it might be useful to be able to talk with Monty in the Wide World."

"Oh, well done, good idea," said Ffain admiringly, I could see Petunia smiling at his praise. The green dragon turned to the mouse.

"Come on then, hop on, we've wasted enough time."

Monty looked at the dragon's scaly neck and hesitated briefly before quickly kicking off his boots and removing his hat and belt; then he threw himself onto Ffain and scrambled towards me.

"I couldn't bring them," he said sadly, craning his neck for one last look of his treasured possessions as Ffain began to move. He moved closer to me and caught hold of the front of my jumper to balance himself.

"I wouldn't be able to grip you see. I hope they'll be okay."

He sounded so sad I felt sorry for him and wanted to cheer him up.

"I'm sure your things will be quite safe and you still look like a superhero without them."

"Really?" Monty grinned up at me. "Monty Super Hero."

"Of course ... woah!"

I made a grab for one of the triangles sticking up

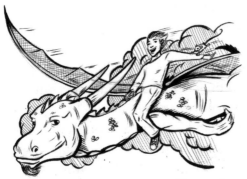

from Ffain's neck as the green dragon spread his wings and took off into the night sky.

"Wow," I said, as the trees below them grew smaller and smaller. "Just look at that! Isn't this great?"

We were following the course of a river, I could see its water reflecting the moonlight and every now and then I caught a glimpse of Sirocco galloping beside it, his mane and tail streaming out in the wind. The air was rushing past my face too. This is so exciting, I thought, this is the most exciting thing I have ever done. I'm so glad I came.

I looked down to say something to Monty; the little mouse was still holding on tight to my jumper but he had curled himself into a ball, his eyes shut tight and the cold night air was ruffling his fur. I cupped one hand around him, gently eased him up and tucked him into the neck of my sweater.

Monty snuggled up against my neck and murmured, "Thank you, I don't think superheroes like heights."

I smiled as I looked across at Petunia flying beside us but the grim look of determination on the purple dragon's face reminded me of the purpose of our journey. Who knew what lay ahead?

Ffain started to lose height and I saw that we had

reached the mouth of the river; I could see the sea sparkling in the moonlight and smell the tang of salt in the air. Ffain glided down and landed on the sand next to Petunia, by the time I had climbed down from the green dragon's back we had been joined by Sirocco. I could feel Monty's whiskers tickling my neck as the mouse peeped out from my collar, peering all around.

"The cave's this way," said Petunia.

Thank goodness for the full moon, I thought, as we followed her across the beach; but I was even more grateful for my torch when we reached the dark mouth of the cave.

"That's marvellous, Edward, well done," Ffain remarked as the strong beam lit the path leading to the portal, and I felt a warm glow at the dragon's praise. The passage through the portal wasn't so bad this time; I put this down to being able to walk through. The back of the cave became narrower and narrower; it was filled with a blackness that even the torch couldn't penetrate. With Monty perched on my shoulder, I approached cautiously, as I stepped slowly into the murky darkness I suddenly found himself shooting forwards, drawn by an irresistible force like iron filings to a magnet. I wasn't aware of moving my legs but all the same I felt myself rushing forwards, whether it was through time or space or both I couldn't tell. The forward movement stopped as abruptly as it had started, the darkness melted away and, the next thing I knew, I was standing on a hillside next to Sirocco and Petunia trying to catch my breath. I looked back over my shoulder and saw Ffain emerge from behind a large slab of rock that was balanced at an angle against the hillside. No passer-by would have given it a second glance.

On our short walk across the beach and into the cave Petunia had explained that she and Mistral had been looking for rowan trees to use in medicine. She had also told me the circumstances that had led to the unicorns' capture, I didn't like the sound of Billy and Dave at all and now I understood the urgency of our mission.

Petunia had mentioned that once upon a time the dragons had visited the Wide World frequently and been good friend with the humans, but then during the time of her grandparents they were banished. I was longing to hear the full story; I couldn't imagine why anyone would want to get rid of the dragons or the unicorns. Petunia had promised to tell me everything as soon as time allowed, but for now all the purple dragon could think of was getting back to her friend. She led us down the hill to the shores of the lake, we could just make out the dark outline of the island at its centre, but there was no sign of the boat.

Petunia started to panic but Ffain raised a calming paw and said, "Now, now they must have put it back so that no one would notice it was missing and come to investigate. Can you remember which direction Dave took when he went to fetch it?"

Petunia took a deep breath to quell her rising panic.

"Yes, I expect you're right, that must be it. It was that way, I think," she pointed to the right and then added. "Yes, I'm sure it was that way and it can't have been far because he wasn't gone that long."

Ffain smiled at her encouragingly. "Well done, now what I suggest is that you fly across and let Mistral know we are here. I'll go with Edward and Sirocco, once we've found the boat, and Edward is safely on his way, I'll come over to let you know, okay?"

"Yes," we all chorused.

Time had passed very slowly for poor Mistral, she imagined Petunia's journey in her head and tried to judge whereabouts the dragon might be and what she may be doing; but it was very difficult. She knew time passed differently in the Wide World but she still felt as though she had been tied up on the island for hours and hours.

She wondered who Petunia would go to for help, her parents, Rufus, Lochinvar, no not Lochinvar, Mistral could remember how furious he had been when his son, Ffain, had broken the dragon's vow and returned to the Wide World. Ffain, of course, Petunia had said that she would go to get him. Mistral smiled, Petunia had a soft spot for Ffain, she would tease her friend about that when she saw her next. If there is a next time, said a gloomy voice in her head, and there certainly won't be if Billy and Dave come back.

No, Mistral shook her head as if to dislodge the thought from her brain. No, she wouldn't think like that, Petunia would come, Petunia was her best friend, she had to come. The unicorn sighed; she just wished the dragon would hurry up.

Mistral tried to pass the time by sleeping but as soon as she closed her eyes she saw Billy, throwing water, laughing at her, calling her 'my beauty' in his horrible, creepy voice; sleep was out of the question.

Where was Petunia now? Was she on her way back yet? Mistral moved around as much as the rope would allow, trying to ease her bruised legs, which were beginning to stiffen up. A few bruises will probably be the least of my worries when I get back, she thought. Compared to the amount of trouble Petunia and I will be in, but I don't care, I just want to get off this island. Get off this island. The words repeated over and over in her head. How on earth *was* she going to get off this island? The unicorn gave another sigh full of hopelessness and despair; she just couldn't see a way out of this mess.

At long last Mistral heard it, the sound she had been longing for, Petunia calling out her name as she flew overhead.

"Oh Petunia, I'm so glad you're back. I can't begin to tell you … but, you're not on your own, are you?"

"No of course not, Ffain and Sirocco are with me. Try not to worry; everything is going to be alright."

"Ffain *and* Sirocco, my goodness; but Petunia how are you going to get me off the island? I just can't see a way of doing it; I've been thinking and thinking ..."

"Ssh, it's okay, you won't believe this but we've brought a boy, a real, live boy. His name is Edward, you'll like him, and he's going to untie you and row you back across."

Mistral couldn't believe what she was hearing.

"A boy! I don't believe it, I don't understand; how ... where did you find a boy?"

"It was Monty. Monty went and fetched him."

"The mouse?!" Mistral said incredulously.

"Yes, and I don't think we are ever going to hear the end of it," Ffain's deep voice boomed out as he joined Petunia. "He and Edward are on their way to you now. Just hold on for a little longer my dear; we'll soon have you out of here."

Mistral fell silent trying to take in what her friends had told her. She listened to the comforting beat of their wings through the air as they hovered over her; it was so good not to be alone anymore.

I must admit I was shocked by the size of the boat; I had never rowed anything that large before. Even so, it wasn't big enough to accommodate two unicorns and Sirocco had reluctantly agreed to stay behind. He knew it made sense, he could see that I was going to struggle with one unicorn in the boat, let alone two; but it didn't make it any easier. He watched as I settled myself on the seat, picked up the oars and sat waiting for him to push the boat out into the water.

"Please bring her back safely," he asked. "And tell her I'm waiting, won't you?"

"I will, I promise," I said solemnly.

Sirocco placed his chest against the end of the boat and gave it a powerful push, then he stood in the shallows watching as it disappeared into the darkness. The last thing he heard was Monty's voice floating back over the water, calling out.

"Never fear my friend; Monty Super Hero will rescue her."

Then there was silence.

The mouse was so excited about travelling in a boat; he had never been in one before. I gave him the job of look out, asking him to sit in the bows, ready to help guide us in as soon as he could see the island. I was glad of Monty's company as I tried not to think too much about what lay ahead but just concentrate on rowing in a steady rhythm and, what I hoped, was a straight line.

"Can I be Captain, Edward, can I, can I?"

"Um, I think it's probably better if I stay in charge of the boat, but you can be First Mate, that's a very important job," I said not wanting to disappoint him. "I need you to keep a look out for the island and make sure we are going in the right direction."

"Aye, aye Captain," said Monty, in what he hoped was a suitably nautical voice.

Where on earth did he learn that? I wondered. The mouse settled down for a while and the only noise was the sound of the oars dipping in and out of the water. Then Monty spoke quietly.

"I think I'm beginning to feel a bit seasick."

"Try just looking straight ahead and not at the water going past," I advised, smiling to myself. What a great superhero, afraid of heights and sea sick, I thought.

"Tell me about rainbow mice, I see you've gone brown again. Does that always happen when you enter the Wide World?"

The distraction worked, Monty chatted away and I learnt about rainbow mice and the Inner World. It wasn't long before the boat slid gently up on the shore of the island and we heard Petunia calling out excitedly to Mistral.

"I can see them, I can see the boat. Edward is just landing it now. They'll be with you soon."

"They? You only mentioned one boy." One boy was bad enough, Mistral wasn't sure she could cope with two.

"There is only one boy, Monty's with him."

Mistral shook her head in astonishment, really that mouse. She could hear Ffain calling out directions and then the sound of someone approaching, pushing through the undergrowth. The bushes beside her parted and there I was, a boy, just an ordinary boy, not half as scary as Billy or Dave.

I smiled at her. "Hello, I'm Edward. I've come to rescue you."

"And me, and me!" It was Monty, standing on my shoulder, grinning from ear to ear. "Told you I was a good rescuer, didn't I?"

Mistral couldn't help but smile back, for the first time in hours she felt a glimmer of hope. She looked me in the eye and obviously decided that I had a kind face.

"I'm really pleased to meet you Edward, and you, you ridiculous creature," she added, laughing at Monty.

"Right then, let's get you untied."

I laid the torch on the ground, took hold of the knot in the rope securing Mistral to the tree and tried to prise it apart, it wouldn't move. I turned it round in my hand and examined it more closely in the beam of the torch, then tucking the torch between my upper arm and my body so the light still shone on the knot, I tried again, it still wouldn't move.

"It's so tight I can't get it undone. Have you been pulling on it?"

"I'm afraid I did a bit," Mistral confessed.

"Don't worry. I can try pulling the halter off, if that's okay?"

Mistral lowered her head and I tried to work my fingers under the rope behind her ears. The halter was so tight I could hardly get it to move and I knew there was no way of loosening it enough to allow it to pass over the unicorn's ears. I felt so angry towards the man who had tied it so tightly to this beautiful creature's head.

"It's so tight it must be hurting you and it won't move I'm afraid. Is it very painful?"

"Well, I won't be sorry to get it off," Mistral admitted.

I tried the knot again and Monty climbed up the tree to take a closer look, it still wouldn't budge.

"If only I had thought to bring a knife," I said.

"What's happening?" Ffain called down. "Is there a problem?"

I explained as I worked and worked at the knot. My fingers were starting to hurt from the roughness of the rope and I could only imagine how tender and sore the soft skin on Mistral's face must be feeling, as she stood patiently beside me waiting to be released.

"Is there any way I could get close enough to burn it?" Ffain asked.

"I don't think so."

I closed my eyes for a moment as I tried to think things through, there had to be a way. I looked up, trying to catch a glimpse of Ffain through the tree tops.

"Supposing you lit a fire somewhere else and I brought a branch back here to burn through it?"

"It could work," said Ffain doubtfully. "But you'd have to make sure you could put out the end of the rope before the whole thing caught fire."

For a moment I had a terrible vision of Mistral, her head covered in flames from the burning halter.

"I know I could take off my T-shirt, soak it in water and hold the end of the rope with that."

"Ahem, excuse me," Mistral nudged me gently on the shoulder. "Shall we go?"

The unicorn stepped away from me and, to my amazement; I saw the end of the rope hanging below her nose.

"How did you manage that?"

"My super hero," said Mistral, making a small upwards motion with her head.

I looked up to see Monty smiling down at me from between the unicorn's ears.

"My mother always told me to look after my teeth."

"Monty you are a marvel!"

"Thank you." The mouse gave a small bow.

"Don't tell me he's done it again," said Ffain with a groan.

"He certainly has," I called back laughing. "Come on, let's go."

But our relief was short lived, for when we got to the shore Mistral froze at the sight of the water and refused to step into the boat.

"I'm sorry, I just can't do it. I can't go in a boat again."

"But you have to there is no other way to get you back," I explained.

"I can't, I just can't," Mistral repeated. "It's the water." She gave a shudder.

"Mistral, you have to do this, there is no other way," Ffain said sternly.

I tried pleading with Mistral again.

"You don't have to get your feet wet. I can hold the boat so that you can step straight in."

"Please, you have to try," begged Monty from his place in the boat.

The unicorn shook her head and planted her feet more firmly on the ground. Petunia spoke to her.

"Mistral, Sirocco is waiting for you. You know what that's like; you had to wait for me to come back. You can imagine what he is going through, what he is thinking."

Mistral stepped towards the boat; I tightened my grip on the side to stop it swinging. I held my breath as the unicorn hesitated, her feet inches away from the water's edge. Petunia spoke again.

"You know he volunteered to go in your place. Sirocco said he would go with the men instead of you. He really cares for you, just think of the life you could have together."

Ffain looked at Petunia with surprise, but everyone else was too busy concentrating on Mistral to notice. The unicorn shut her eyes and raised one foreleg.

"Help me Edward, please."

Hoping the boat wouldn't move too much, I

stretched out my hand, clasped the unicorn's leg firmly and guided it into the bottom of the boat.

"Now the other one," I prompted. "That's it almost there. Take a step forward and I'll help you with the back ones."

Mistral, her eyes still tightly shut, gave a gasp as she felt the boat move under her weight, for one dreadful moment I thought she was going to leap back out.

"That's the way," Monty sang out. "All aboard the good ship 'Rescuer', Captain Edward and First Mate Monty in charge, it's the only way to travel."

"Oh Monty," Mistral almost laughed as she took a nervous step forward. "You are incorrigible."

"That's a long word," remarked Monty. "I'll have to look that one up in the dictionary."

That was when I realised what had been going on, the mouse must have been reading my books and my comics; that would explain a lot. I made a mental note to ask him about it later as I gently placed first one and then the other of Mistral's hind legs in the boat; and then hurried to get the boat under way before the unicorn could change her mind.

Ffain and Petunia flew on to let Sirocco know that we were finally on our way. I watched Mistral closely as she stood trembling in the middle of the boat. I didn't speak until I was sure we were far enough away from the island for it to be impossible for her to try jumping out then, remembering the trip across with Monty, I asked.

"Can you tell me more about the history of the dragons and the unicorns, please Mistral. Petunia told me a little but I would love to hear more and it would help to pass the time."

There was a pause before Mistral begun to speak, she was hesitant at first, but her voice gradually became more confident as she related the story to me, I could see her relax a little but her eyes still remained tightly shut. Despite being fascinated by what I was hearing I concentrated on my rowing, trying to get across the lake as quickly as possible. Aware that it had taken much longer to get Mistral off the island than we had expected, I strained against the oars, pushing my tired body on, knowing time was beginning to run out. I felt a wave of relief wash over me when Monty finally called out.

"We're almost there, I can see them."

Then I felt my relief turn to dread as the mouse added in a horrified whisper.

"Oh no! Edward you'd better take a look at this."

I lifted the oars and looked over my shoulder as the boat floated towards the shore. I could see Ffain and Petunia standing to one side, Sirocco next to them, then I felt my stomach flip over, standing beside the unicorn were two men and one of them was holding a gun to Sirocco's head. As the boat grounded on the stony shallows the other man came forward and caught hold of the bows pulling it further up onto the shore.

"Thanks a lot mate," he said to me. "Saved us a job. What did I tell yer Dave," he shouted back over his shoulder. "I knew 'e was lying, looks like we got ourselves a matching set, gold and silver."

Mistral's eyes flew open at the sound of Billy's voice

and she sprang out of the boat nearly tipping Monty and me into the water, but the man was too quick for her, he leapt forward and caught hold of the end of the rope almost before her hooves touched the ground.

"Hello again my beauty, nice of you to join us."

As he turned to lead the unicorn away I jumped over the side of the boat and rushed at Billy, I threw myself on his back and tried to punch him in the face.

Billy fell down under my weight and the two of us rolled on the ground, a tangle of arms and legs. Mistral jerked herself free and turned ready to give the man a kick as soon as the opportunity presented itself. Billy was stronger and heavier than me, he soon managed to toss me to one side. Then he caught hold of me by the throat and dragged me up onto my knees; he didn't see Mistral begin to lift her hind leg.

A shot rang out causing the unicorn to jump with shock and her leg fell harmlessly to the ground. She looked across to the others; Dave had the gun back against Sirocco's head.

"The next one's for 'im," he said menacingly. "Makes no difference to me wevver 'es alive or dead."

Billy dragged me up onto my feet and slapped me hard across the head, making me stagger.

"Cheeky little beggar, 'bout time someone put you in your place."

I put my hand up to my ringing ear, I could feel tears pricking at the back of my eyes and I swallowed hard determined not to let Billy see me cry. I sneaked a look at him and saw he had a trickle of blood coming from his nose; that made me feel better. Billy turned to take hold of Mistral's rope again and as he did Monty ran swiftly up the outside of my jeans and jumper and tucked himself into my collar. I must say the warmth of the little mouse's body next to my skin was very reassuring. Then Billy grabbed me roughly by the arm and dragged me and the unicorn over to the others.

"Are you alright Mistral?" Sirocco asked.

"Yes, I'm okay," she replied smiling at him. "Thank you for coming, I'm sorry about …"

"It's all my fault, I should never have let you come," Petunia interrupted her friend, her green eyes brimming with tears.

Ffain laid a consoling paw on the purple dragon's shoulder but before he could say anything Billy spoke.

"Very touching I'm sure, now shut up the lot of yer and let me fink."

I looked at Ffain, he was regarding Billy with such contempt and hatred in his yellow eyes, that I knew I wouldn't want to be in Billy's shoes, only the gun aimed at Sirocco's head was holding the green dragon back. Even in the moonlight I thought I could detect a faint wisp of smoke curling up from Ffain's nostrils.

"What we gonna do wiv this lot then?" asked Dave.

I watched him closely, trying to work out whether

or not it was worth rushing at him and trying to make him drop the gun. No, he would pull the trigger and shoot Sirocco, I was sure of it. If only there was a way of getting hold of the gun. I glanced across at Ffain again; he too was staring intently at Dave. The dragon felt my eyes on him and met my gaze, he gave a small shake of his head as if to say, 'Not yet, but be ready'. Then he turned his attention back to Dave, the man became aware that the dragon was staring at him and shifted uneasily from foot to foot.

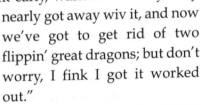

"Watcha looking at, yer evil, old lizard," he shouted up at Ffain, who carried on regarding him menacingly. "C'mon Billy boy make yer mind up, this bloomin' fing's giving me the creeps."

"Yeah, well, it's them that's the problem innit?" said Billy, jabbing his thumb in the direction of the dragons. "Mind you, good job we came back early, wasn't it? Blimey, they nearly got away wiv it, and now we've got to get rid of two flippin' great dragons; but don't worry, I fink I got it worked out."

"What about the kid? I aint murdering no kid."

Murder! I felt a cold sweat break out over my body

and my legs suddenly went weak, I tried not to let Billy feel me tremble.

"Nah, don't worry about 'im, 'e can go for a nice, long trip in the boat wivout any oars." Billy sniggered. "That'll keep 'im out of the way, by the time anyone finds 'im, we'll be long gone. Besides, who's gonna believe a kid telling 'em there was dragons? We'll 'ave an 'ard enough job convincing everyone them unicorns is real. Nah, they'll just fink 'es doolally." Billy made circular motions by the side of his head with one finger. "'Ere, we still got all that rope you nicked in the lorry?"

"Yeah," Dave smirked.

"That's it then, I'll get the rope and the spare can of diesel, we'll tie the two of 'em up and have ourselves a nice bonfire."

A wave of shock swept over my body as I realised what Billy meant to do. At first I felt as though there was ice running through my veins, then in a flash I was red hot with anger, angrier than I had ever been in my life.

"You can't do that, I won't let you!" I shouted furiously.

Wrenching my arm out of Billy's fist I dropped my head and launched myself at him as fast as I could, butting him hard in the stomach.

"Oof!" The man dropped to the ground with a thump as the breath was knocked out of his body. I fell forward onto my hand and knees, between the two men and Dave aimed a vicious kick at my ribs. Although I was unaware of it at the time, Monty seized his chance and jumped from my neck onto Dave's leg.

Finding herself free from Billy's grasp Mistral spun

round, and kicking out with both hind legs, hit him squarely in the back just as he started to get to his feet. As Billy fell forwards, flat on his face, Dave let out a tremendous howl of pain as Monty bit him in the hand, he dropped the gun and as it hit the ground it fired shooting Billy in the leg.

Billy screamed and rolled around on the ground in agony clutching his injured leg. Dave and I both dived for the gun at the same time, just as it seemed he was going to get there first a mighty swipe from Ffain's forepaw sent Dave flying through the air, he came crashing down on top of the injured Billy making him yelp with pain.

I got to my feet and, clasping the gun in both hands, aimed it at the pair of them. Billy lay whimpering on the ground with his eyes closed; both hands clasped tightly around one thigh, I could see blood oozing between his fingers. Dave sat up and eyed me warily.

"Come off it, who are yer trying to kid, you aint gonna shoot us."

"Don't bet on it," I said as bravely as I could, but even as I spoke I wasn't sure I could carry out the threat.

"He doesn't need to, he's got us," Ffain reminded Dave, as he and Petunia stepped up and stood either side of me.

"And us," Sirocco and Mistral spoke together as they came to stand on either side of the three of us.

The man looked at the two huge dragons and the unicorns flanking me, he swallowed hard.

"Watcha gonna do?" he asked nervously.

"Now let me see, what was it you were going to do to us?" Ffain pretended to think. "Oh yes, you were going to burn us alive and cut off my friend's horns, after you'd beaten them of course."

Dave sank to his knees, next to the moaning Billy, and held up his clasped his hands.

"No, no, please don't do that," he begged.

Even in the moonlight I could see how pale the man had gone, I tried to hold the gun steady and not show how shocked I was at Ffain's words; surely he wouldn't? But I couldn't help giving the dragon a startled glance when I heard what he said next.

"Take off your jacket and shirt."

Dave looked at the green dragon in open mouthed horror.

"N-no," he stammered. "Please."

Ffain stepped forwards threateningly. "Just do it."

"No Ffain, don't."

I tried to run forward but Petunia laid a restraining paw on my shoulder.

"It's alright," she whispered. "Just wait."

Under Ffain's menacing yellow eyed stare Dave reluctantly took off his jacket and shirt and stood in front of the dragon bare-chested. I could see the man's skin puckered with goose bumps from fear and cold, and felt myself shiver in sympathy. What was Ffain playing at? I didn't want to watch what Ffain did next, but I couldn't look away either. I held my breath as the green dragon stepped right up to Dave, without taking his eyes from the man's face; he bent down, picked up the shirt and tore it into shreds. Dave gasped out loud as the material ripped like tissue paper in the dragon's talons. Still with his terrible yellow eyes fixed on the man's face, Ffain held the remains of the shirt out to one side.

"Petunia," he said calmly.

Dave and I watched in astonishment as the purple dragon stepped forward, took the strips of material from Ffain's paw and, bending over Billy, began to gently but firmly bandage his injured leg.

"Better put your jacket back on," Ffain smiled at the open mouthed Dave. "You don't want to catch a chill, do you?"

Dave dumbly did as he was told. I felt weak with relief; Sirocco looked at my face and smiled.

"You didn't really think he'd do it, did you? He is a dragon of honour, you know, and bound by oaths."

I was speechless, I shook my head in admiration at the way the green dragon had handled the situation.

"How does it look, Petunia?" Ffain asked.

"Luckily the bullet passed straight through his leg. I've bound it up tightly and it's already almost stopped bleeding. I'm afraid he'll live, mores the pity."

"Petunia, I'm shocked, and you a healer." Ffain rebuked her, but I could hear the laughter in his voice. The green dragon turned back to Dave.

"Right, where were we? Oh yes, the list of things you were going to do to us." He nodded at Billy. "Get him up on his feet, and then both of you get in the boat."

Dave put one of Billy's arms round his neck and dragged him upright; he supported him, limping and moaning over to the boat, where he helped him in.

"And I believe," said Fain as he followed them. "That this is what you were going to do to my good friend Edward. I'll have those, thank you very much."

The dragon neatly flicked the oars out of the boat and onto the stones as if they weighed no more than a couple of matchsticks. Then with a mighty push he sent the boat skimming away over the lake.

"Enjoy your trip, gentlemen," he called out as it disappeared from sight and Billy's moans of pain faded into the night.

Ffain came back to us dusting off his paws.

"It's over," he announced. "Well done everyone, especially you Edward, you were very brave. Are you alright?"

I felt my heart swell with pride at the dragon's praise.

"Yes," I said. "Just a bit bruised, but if it hadn't been for Monty biting Dave ..."

"Monty!"

We all looked at each other in horror as we realised none of us had seen the mouse since the fight.

"Dave threw up his hand when he bit him and made him drop the gun," said Sirocco. "I think he may have thrown him up in the air, something came flying past my head but I didn't realise ..."

The unicorn's voice trailed off, we were all stunned into silence as we thought about what may have happened to the mouse.

"Come on," Ffain urged us into action. "We've got to find him before we go. We must take him back with us even if ..."

He didn't wait to finish the sentence but marched away up the lakeside calling out Monty's name. The others quickly followed suit. I ran back to where I had last seen the torch laying amongst the stones, hoping desperately it was still working. I was immensely relieved when the beam shone out at the first flick of the switch. I started walking, shining the torch from side to side and calling out Monty's name as I went. All around me I could hear the others doing the same thing.

"Monty, Monty. Where are you?"

Of all the dreadful things that had happened that night this was the worst. In my mind's eye I could see the little mouse standing so proudly in his ridiculous boots and hat, giving a little bow, 'Monty Action Mouse, at your service'.

"Monty, Monty. Where are you?"

I remembered the comforting feeling of the mouse's body curled up against my neck. He had to be alive, he just had to be.

"Monty, Monty. Where are you?"

I heard the mouse's voice in my head, 'All aboard the good ship 'Rescuer', Captain Edward and First Mate Monty in charge'. He had been such good company, always cheerful, never complaining, just getting on with what needed to be done.

I shook my head angrily, whatever was I thinking 'had been'. No. It couldn't be true, I wouldn't let it be true, I was going to find Monty and he was going to be alright.

"Monty, Monty. Where are you?"

At first I thought it was an old leaf, but as I turned away I remembered it was only September and I quickly swung the torch back for a second look. A light breeze blew over the object and I saw fur ruffling.

"Over here! Over here, I've found him!"

The others arrived as I was bending down to cup my hands around the mouse's body.

"Careful Edward," warned Petunia. "Try to move him as little as possible."

The warm body felt impossibly light in my hands as I held them out towards Petunia. Ffain held the torch as she gently examined Monty. The mouse didn't move and there was a strained silence as we all waited for her to speak.

"It's difficult to tell," she said at last. "He's obviously had a blow on the head, but I don't think there are any bones broken and his breathing seems okay. All we can do is keep him warm and get him back to the sanctuary as soon as possible. My mother will know what to do."

"If only he had been wearing his hat," Mistral said sadly.

I tucked Monty inside my collar and the five of us made our way silently back up the hill to the portal as quickly as we could. The joy we had all felt at defeating Billy and Dave was gone.

Petunia retrieved the precious, young rowan trees from their hiding place and gave a deep sigh as she looked at them in her paw. Had it really been worth it? Ffain placed his paw on top of hers and gave it a reassuring squeeze.

"Come on, let's go home."

PART 5. HOME IS WHERE THE HEART IS

X

I would have enjoyed the trip back a lot more if I hadn't been so worried about Monty. We had emerged from the cave on the beach into bright sunshine and, from my vantage point on Ffain's back, I had a wonderful view of the Inner World. I just wished Monty had been there beside me pointing out the sights instead of curled up, unmoving, beneath the collar of my jumper.

We were following the river again, upstream this

time. I watched Ffain's and Petunia's shadows flickering over the tops of the trees below us. I saw a large bend ahead in the river and felt the green dragon begin to descend. This must be it. I put up my hand and laid my fingers lightly on the precious bulge under my collar and, closing my eyes, took a couple of deep breaths. A combination of worry and exhaustion was keeping my nerves on edge, I glanced across at Petunia, the concerned expression on the purple dragon's face as she prepared to land did nothing to allay my fears.

"Petunia, where on earth have you been? Your father and I have been so worried about you."

Another purple dragon, an older version of Petunia, came hurrying across to meet us. I was interested to see a white hare trotting along beside her, a nippy, I had heard about them.

"And Ffain as well, and ...oh," Lavender caught sight of me. "What *is* going on?"

"I'll explain later Mama, I promise, but right now we need your help."

Petunia turned to the nippy and thrust the young rowan trees she had been carrying into his paws.

"Take these to Papa please Chalky; he'll know what to do with them."

The hare shook his head in wonder at the plants as he obediently set off to find Horatio.

"Edward?"

I had climbed stiffly down from Ffain's back and was standing looking around in astonishment at the grassy meadow formed by the river bend. I could see various creatures lying and sitting in the shade of the willow trees, whilst the nippies trotted in and out from a large cave set in the nearby hills, tending to their needs. There were a few unicorns, one with a patch over one eye, several species of beautifully coloured birds and even a nippy sitting alone, looking sorry for itself, one paw heavily bandaged.

Despite the number of creatures around it was a very peaceful place, the air smelt of fresh grass, herbs and flowers. I breathed in slowly, savouring the aroma, and immediately felt calmer. I couldn't quite work out what it was but something about the place just felt right.

"Edward, are you alright?"

The sound of Petunia's voice brought me out of my reverie and I looked round to see the three dragons regarding me with concern. Lavender stepped over to me, placed one forepaw gently on my shoulder and, looking deep into my eyes, she asked.

"You feel it, don't you? That this is a special place, a place of healing."

I looked up at her wise face and nodded.

"It feels like coming home, doesn't it?" the dragon continued, smiling at me.

"Yes," I returned her smile. That was exactly it; Lavender had described what I had been feeling perfectly.

"It will always be here, wherever you go, whatever you do, you can always come back here whenever you need to. It's a comforting thought, isn't it?"

I nodded again.

"I believe there is someone else who could benefit from the sanctuary's magic."

Lavender held out her paw and I felt a sinking feeling in my stomach as I realised the moment I had been dreading had arrived. I lifted Monty from my jumper and laid him carefully on the dragon's paw. The mouse didn't stir; his fur was a strange colour, brown with a faint bluish tinge.

"He's not … he's not …" I could not make myself say that terrible word. I was afraid that if I actually said it, it would be true, Lavender understood.

"No, he's still alive," she assured me. "I've seen this odd colouring before when one of the rainbow mice comes back from the Wide World with an injury. He has had a nasty bump on the head though, but his body is doing the right thing, keeping him asleep while it heals itself. I shall take him up to the cave to treat him. You can come up later. It looks as though you've got a few bumps and bruises yourself that need seeing to."

"I'll attend to those, Mama," Petunia came over and stood beside me. "Mistral will be here soon with Sirocco, I'm afraid she needs some first aid too. We flew on ahead because we were worried about Monty."

"The unicorns as well, whatever have you been up to? I shall expect to hear the full story later."

With that Lavender turned on her heels and carried Monty away to the cave. I could hear her calling out orders to the nippies as she went.

"Will you be in a lot of trouble?" I asked Petunia.

"I expect so."

She gave a small sigh as she led me over to one of the willow trees. Beneath its shady branches lay a thick mattress of grass and herbs. Petunia told me  to lie down and, much to my surprise I discovered it to be the most comfortable, and certainly the most fragrant, bed I had ever used. A nippy arrived beside us bearing a loaded tray and Petunia skilfully began to bathe my bruises.

I closed my eyes and tried to identify the various scents, as the witch hazel the dragon was using soothed my aching body. I could recognise lavender and rosemary, I knew them from my parents' garden, and there was something else that reminded me of my mother's kitchen, thyme, yes, that was it. It was the first time I had thought about Mum and Dad, I wondered drowsily if they were missing me. I was vaguely aware of being propped up, someone holding a cup to my lips and urging me to drink. I obeyed sleepily and felt a comforting warmth slide down my throat and into my body as I drifted off into blissful sleep.

By the time I woke the sun was low in the sky and the day was almost over. I was lying on my side, someone had tucked a blanket over me and I felt snug and safe. What a wonderful place, what a marvellous bed, and I could come whenever I wanted, Lavender had said so. 'It will always be here,' she had said; it gave me a warm glow inside just to think of it. I turned on my back, stretched luxuriously, and gave a contented sigh.

"Oh good you're awake. Are you feeling better?"

The voice came from right beside the bed and made me jump. It was a nippy.

"Sorry, I didn't mean to startle you. Are you feeling quite well? Only the others are wondering if you'd like to join them. I'm Chalky by the way."

It was the same hare I had seen earlier, I was glad he had told me his name, they all looked so alike. I wondered which question to answer first.

"Yes, thank you. Pleased to meet you Chalky. Where are the others?"

"They're waiting for you up at the cave. They won't start the storytelling without you."

Storytelling? Mistral had mentioned the dragon's tradition of storytelling but I couldn't understand why they were doing it now unless ..., a thought struck me.

"Are we the story? I mean what we did?"

"Yes, of course. Now come along Sir, I'll show you the way."

With a terrible jolt I remembered something else.

"How's Monty, do you know? Is he alright?"

"You'd better see for yourself, come along," said Chalky setting off at a trot, and leaving me with no choice but to quickly get my shoes back on and hurry after him.

The area in front of the cave was buzzing with activity; I paused at the edge of the clearing trying to take it all in. Two large tables had been placed to one side and a stream of nippies were scurrying to and fro laying out plates of food on them under the direction of a red dragon. My mouth began to water at the sight of the food making me realise how hungry I was.

A large pit had been dug in the centre of the clearing and filled with firewood, standing beside it were four dragons, one red, one purple and two green, one of the green ones was Ffain. The red dragon looked up, saw me, and gave Ffain a nudge, nodding in my direction.

"Ah, Edward, there you are," Ffain came hurrying across. "Feeling better after your sleep, I hope. Everyone's very anxious to meet you. Come along."

The dragon turned to the nippy. "It's okay Chalky, thank you. I'll take care of Mr. Edward now, I'm sure you've got a lot to do."

I followed Ffain over to the three dragons feeling rather nervous, even though I knew they would do me no harm, it was quite scary to find myself surrounded by the huge creatures. Ffain introduced Rufus and Horatio. Rufus was the red dragon and it was his wife Ariadne that I had seen supervising the feast, he smiled down at me in a kindly manner and I began to feel less afraid.

Horatio the purple dragon was, of course, Petunia's father, he appeared to be very old and leant heavily on a walking stick. As he bent down to shake my hand I could see where Petunia got her striking green eyes from.

"Proud to meet you young man, I look forward to talking with you later and catching up on all that's been happening in the Wide World since I was last there."

"And this," Ffain concluded. "Is my father, Lochinvar, ruler of the High Mountain."

If Petunia got her eyes from her father it was obvious to see where Ffain got his commanding presence from, Lochinvar was the most magnificent creature I had ever seen. I wondered whether I should bow or kneel but before I could do either the dragon spoke.

"Edward, I believe we owe you a great debt of gratitude. Ffain has been telling us about your bravery and resourcefulness and I look forward to hearing your story. The misunderstanding between people and dragons has been a great sadness to all of us; it's good to have some human company again. I hope you enjoy your stay and I hope it will be the first of many. You will always be welcome here."

My heart filled with joy at Lochinvar's words, I felt so happy I was almost speechless.

"Th-thank you Sir," I managed to stammer as the green dragon shook me warmly by the hand.

"And now," said Ffain. "I must take Edward away for a few moments; there is someone I know he wants to see before the celebrations begin."

The dragon led me towards the mouth of the cave, stopped just outside, and said, "You go on in, come and re-join us whenever you're ready."

Ffain turned to go back to the others and left me standing anxiously by the cave entrance. I desperately wanted to see Monty but now I was there I was worried about what state I was going to find the mouse in. I swallowed hard, summoned up my courage, and took another couple of steps forwards. I heard a voice coming from inside the cave.

"So then I said, 'My mother always told me to look after my teeth.'"

This was followed by a burst of giggling and someone saying, "Ooh Monty, you are a one."

"Monty?"

I rushed into the cave and discovered Monty sitting up in bed, a bandage round his head, bright blue fur gleaming in the candlelight. A golden yellow mouse was perched on the end of his bed, laughing.

"Edward!"

"Monty, I can't believe it, you're alright, you're really alright. Oh, it's wonderful to see you."

I knelt down beside the bed, overcome with happiness, almost unable to believe what I was seeing with my own eyes. Monty grinned at me.

"It's good to see you too, Captain Edward."

I regarded him anxiously.

"Are you really okay? You were unconscious for quite a long time."

"I'm fine honestly, just a slight headache, and Lavender says that will go soon," he gave a sigh.

"Though I'm afraid she won't let me out of bed to join the storytelling."

"Never mind I'll keep you company," said the golden mouse.

"Will you?" asked Monty, looking a lot more cheerful. "Thank you. Edward, I'd like to introduce Millie. What do you think, eh, Millie and Monty, we make quite a pair don't we?"

"I think you make a great pair," I said, as Millie giggled with embarrassment. "After all, every superhero has to have a partner."

"Did you hear that Mill?" asked Monty. "How do you fancy being partners with a superhero?"

This made Millie giggle even more, her ears flushed pink and she fussed around Monty's bed, tucking in the blankets, to hide her embarrassment.

"Actually, I was thinking I might give up the rescuing," Monty remarked casually. "It's a bit ... um ...a bit ..."

Frightening and terrifying were the two words that sprang into my mind, but I realised Monty didn't want to lose face in front of Millie, so I said, "Exhausting?"

"Yes, that's it, exhausting," said Monty, giving me a grateful look.

"Exciting too, of course," I pointed out.

"Oh, of course," Monty nodded in agreement. "Exciting, but very tiring; and I'm not getting any younger, maybe it's about time I thought of settling down."

He gave Millie a sidelong glance, but she seemed to be busy removing a piece of fluff from the bed.

"You will come to see me sometimes though, won't you?" I asked. "I'm sure there must still be some books on my shelves you haven't read."

Now it was Monty's turn to look embarrassed.

"Don't worry, I don't mind," I said with a chuckle. "But please promise me you'll come, both of you."

The two mice solemnly promised they would and I left them discussing their plans for the future, my heart feeling much lighter than it had when I had first approached the cave.

On my return to the fireside I found all the dragons, including Ffain's mother, Phaedre, and Magenta to whom I was introduced, and Sirocco and Mistral, waiting for me. At first I felt a little awkward, being at the centre of so much attention, but I needn't have worried the dragons soon made me feel at home. Lochinvar formally welcomed everyone to the storytelling and urged us to help ourselves to the food. When I saw the platters of fruit and pies and cakes piled up on the table I suddenly realised how hungry I was, and I didn't need much urging from Ariadne to fill up a plate with cherry pie, chocolate cake, macaroons and a small pile of marshmallows.

The dragons were pleased and excited to have a

human to talk with again, and all of them were anxious to hear what had happened in the Wide World during their long absence; but first they wanted to hear the full account of what had taken place the previous night. I soon realised there was a traditional way the stories were recounted, so I listened politely and waited to be told when it was my turn.

Petunia began the proceedings as she had been the one who had started it all. She explained that all she had planned to do was gather some rowan bark and berries for her parents and come straight back. No one was supposed to ask questions until the tale had been told, but it was obvious that everybody had been very curious about the portal, when Petunia recalled her and Mistral's meeting with Monty and that he had told them about the cave, several of the adult dragons shook their heads in dismay and I heard Lavender murmur, "Those mice, such naughty creatures."

When Petunia had finished Mistral told her version of the story and they learnt how she had been captured by Billy and Dave, which provoked more mutterings of disapproval and of her long wait on the island for her rescuers to come.

Then Ffain told the story of his involvement and Sirocco explained how Billy and Dave had crept up on him while he waited, and held him at gunpoint. With each telling the story grew in depth and the whole picture of the night's happenings became clearer. I could hear how everyone added something as they told their version and I realised that, in a world where there didn't appear to be any books, the telling and

retelling o
stronger, ar
dragon histo.

By the time it
nervous, I stood up .
that had taken place a.
make sure I mentioned M
out that, if the mouse hadn't *the memory*
and made him drop the gun, thi.
out very differently. *of*

With the story finished everyone be.
ask questions at once, I heard Magenta say ...unia,
"Really Tunie, I might have known anything you
organised would be a disaster."

"But it wasn't though, was it?" Mistral spoke up in
defence of her friend. "We all got back safely and
Lavender and Horatio got their rowan trees and
berries."

"But when you think of what could have happened,"
Magenta gave a shudder. "It just doesn't bear thinking
about. Whatever will you get up to next?"

"Oh, I think I'll probably stay around for a while,"
Petunia said casually looking across at Ffain. The green
dragon became aware of her gaze, and the two of them
exchanged a smile.

Horatio approached me.

"Now, young man, if you don't mind I'd like to ask
you some questions," the purple dragon smiled down
at me. "It's been many years since I last travelled in the
Wide World. I hear rumours you have had some terrible
times, times of famine and war."

umpet and honey I
...ed it down with some
...ying to remember my history

...reed. "There have been a lot of wars, in
...ways seems to be one going on somewhere
...world."

"You humans," the old dragon shook his head sadly.
"I don't think I will ever understand you, why can't
you be happy with what you've got and live together
peacefully?"

"Um, I don't know Sir," I said truthfully.

"Inventive bunch though, I'll give you that. I expect
you've got all sorts of wonderful machines these days."

I tried very hard to imagine what the world must
have been like the last time Horatio had visited. How
many hundreds of years ago had it been?

"We've been to
the moon," I said.
"In a rocket."

I heard a strange
rumbling noise
coming from
Horatio and the
old dragon began
to tremble. I took a
step backwards and looked at him with concern; then I
glanced around at the others wondering if I should call
for help. The blast of hot air that burst from Horatio as
he finally started to laugh nearly knocked me off my
feet.

"Ha,ha,ha, been to the moon!" the dragon wheezed, as tears rolled down his face and wisps of smoke drifted from his nostrils. "Been to the moon indeed, even if you could, why would anyone want to?"

"I-I don't know Sir," I stammered.

"Good joke young man, good joke," Horatio patted me on the shoulder as he began to recover. "That's what I've always liked about you humans, your sense of humour. Must go and tell the others, they'll appreciate a good laugh."

The purple dragon wandered over to Rufus and Lochinvar and very soon the sound of three huge dragons laughing was rolling round the fireside.

"Whatever did you say to Papa?"

Petunia asked, as she and Ffain came over to join me.

"It must have been a good joke; I haven't seen him so jolly in a long time."

Wanting to change the subject I asked.

"Are these all of the dragons that live in the Inner World?"

"No," replied Ffain. "There are other dragons that live far away in different areas, but this is all of us from the Kingdom of the High Mountain, except for Aralu, of course."

"Who is Aralu?" I asked.

"Actually, I'm rather glad you asked me that," said Ffain with a rueful smile. "I was hoping I would get the opportunity to speak to you and Petunia without the others overhearing. I've been talking with Sirocco and he agrees that if we are going to be true friends," he smiled down at me and then, looking at Petunia, added. "And if we are going to have any future together, there can be no secrets between us. I have something I need to tell you both and I'm afraid it may make you both change your opinion of me."

Petunia and I wondered what on earth Ffain was about to tell us as he led us away from the gathering towards the river. Once he was sure he couldn't be overheard the green dragon told us the whole story of his trip to see Lucifer, his swearing of the Oath of the White Dragon and his part in the war between the lions and the unicorns.

I, of course, had heard none of it before and found the whole tale extremely thrilling, I was very excited and curious to hear about the battle on Dragon Hill and decided there and then that I would go to visit the site as soon as possible.

"What a wonderful story, thank you for telling me. I think you were very brave to go and help the unicorns. You did what you had to do; I can't see what is wrong with that"

"Thank you Edward, but as time has passed I have come to realise that some of my actions were rather selfish. I was young and hot headed and wanted to make myself a hero without thinking about the consequences, Petunia?"

Ffain regarded the purple dragon anxiously, she had listened in silence as he had told his story and hadn't spoken since. After thinking things through for a little longer she finally spoke.

"Who is to say whether or not what you did, or

what I did, was right or wrong? I acted selfishly too, I wanted everyone to stop thinking I was a foolish, worthless dragon." She held up a paw to silence Ffain as he went to speak. "No, it's true, I know what everyone thought of me and I know why I did what I did, and my actions nearly cost my best friend her life. But, and I believe it is an important but, Ffain, you helped to save hundreds of lives and I have brought an important medicinal plant to the Inner World. We have met Edward and re-established contact with the human race. If no one ever tried to do the things that everyone else says can't be done, both worlds would be a sadder place, don't you think? As for the oath, I believe at the time you genuinely felt as though you had no choice, we will not know the consequences of what you did for a long time, maybe there won't be any, who knows; but if there are I hope we can face them together."

Petunia smiled up at Ffain at the end of what had probably been the longest speech of her life. I took the opportunity to slip quietly away and leave the two dragons alone for a while; they obviously had a lot to talk about. I took a few moments to sit by myself thinking of all I had heard and seen since I had left my bedroom two nights ago; it was a lot to take in. I felt extremely privileged to have discovered this magical place and the creatures that lived there. I was saddened by the thought that I wouldn't be able to share it with any of my friends, Billy and Dave's behaviour had made it quite clear that the Inner World had to remain a secret from most of mankind. But I was full of joy at the thought that I would be able to come back to visit whenever I wanted. There was a lot more of the Inner World to explore, who knew what adventures were waiting for me?

EPILOGUE

Edward stretched out his legs and looked round at his family, Sally was staring into the fireplace lost in thought, Toby and Sox were looking at him expectantly.

"Well, that's it really," he said. "There's not much more to tell. When I got back everything was just as I'd left it, hardly any time had passed at all, just as you discovered Toby."

"Did you go back, Dad?"

"Yes, many times, I never saw Horatio again though, I'm afraid he passed away not long after my first visit.

'Went to live with the Old Ones', that's what you say, isn't Sox?"

"Yes, that's right Mr. Edward. Some dragons believe they still come to the storytelling and sit amongst us round the fire to hear the old tales."

"What a nice thought," remarked Edward. "Are you alright Sally?"

"Yes," his wife replied. "I was just trying to take it all in. What an adventure you had and you were only ten. It's almost unbelievable; but I don't understand why you never told me or anyone else about it before."

Edward smiled. "For that very reason, it is unbelievable. I must admit as a child it was nice to have somewhere that only I could go, it made it even more special, as if it belonged to just me. Sadly, of course, in the end as I got bigger I had to stop going. I just couldn't fit through the tunnel anymore. When I got older and met you it had been so many years, it was almost as if it had all been a dream, and by then I was so used to its being my secret, I confess I never even really thought about telling you. Would you have believed me, if I had?"

"I'm not sure," Sally admitted.

"Don't forget I couldn't have found a way to prove it to you. None of the dragons or unicorns could fit through the tunnel, and if I had shown you a rainbow mouse, bearing in mind it looks just like a normal mouse when it is here, you probably would have screamed and run away."

"You're probably right," Sally laughed.

"When Toby was born, well, that changed

everything. I just knew that if he had my old bedroom one day something would happen, but I must admit I never imagined Sox coming through the tunnel." Edward smiled at the little dragon who had become such an important part of his family.

"I can't believe you had an Action Man," Toby said with a chuckle. "Honestly Dad, they are so lame."

"You have to remember we didn't have home computers then or Xboxes," Edward said in his defence.

"We know what happened to everyone except Monty; did he and Millie come to see you?" Toby asked.

"Oh yes, many times and we read lots of books together, mainly adventure stories, those were his favourite. Years later when I visited them I would hear him repeating them to his children but always with Monty Action Mouse taking the part of the hero." Edward smiled at the memory. "Mistral was right, he was incorrigible."

There was few moments' contented silence as they all thought about the stories they had heard and their friends in the Inner World.

"There is one other thing," said Sox with a frown. "Lucifer and the oath my father gave to him, what is going to happen about that?"

"To be honest with you Sox," said Edward with a sigh. "I've no idea, but I don't believe it is over yet, none of us knows what the future may bring."